Adachi and Shimamura

STORY BY **Hitoma Iruma** ART BY **Non**

NOVEL **7**

"So...what are you doing here at the crack of dawn?"
"I...I thought maybe we could...go to school together..."

Adachi

She has a slim, stick-figure body type with few curves to speak of. She confessed her feelings for Shimamura, and now they're officially a couple, so of course, she's panicking.

"Good morning..."
"I...I'm really
looking forward
to this!"

Shimamura

A girl with a bit of a
ditzy side. As the fall
semester approaches,
she's been contemplating
her new romantic
relationship with Adachi,
but it hasn't sunk in yet.

I had a dream.
It was so awesome,
I couldn't even remember
what happened.
But whatever it was,
it was AWESOME.

I had a dream where I was riding on top of a giant Yashiro-zilla, soaring through the stars. It was fun.

"'Sup."

"Were you, uh, running late today?"

"I kinda overslept."

"Ah."

"I'm just not a morning person."

"Gotcha."

"If you've got nowhere to go, wanna walk to town with me?"

"That sounds nice."

"Say, what's your name?"

Table of Contents

ADACHI TO SHIMAMURA VOL. 7

© Hitoma Iruma 2016
Edited by Dengeki Bunko
Illustrations by Non

First published in Japan in 2016 by
KADOKAWA CORPORATION, Tokyo.
English translation rights arranged with
KADOKAWA CORPORATION, Tokyo.

Seven Seas press and purchase enquiries can be sent to
Marketing Manager Lianne Sentar at press@gomanga.com.
Information regarding the distribution and purchase of
digital editions is available from Digital Manager CK Russell
at digital@gomanga.com.

Follow Seven Seas Entertainment online at
sevenseasentertainment.com.

TRANSLATION: Molly Lee
COVER DESIGN: Nicky Lim
LOGO DESIGN: George Panella
INTERIOR LAYOUT & DESIGN: Clay Gardner
COPY EDITOR: Meg van Huygen
PROOFREADER: B. Lillian Martin
LIGHT NOVEL EDITOR: Nibedita Sen
PRINT MANAGER: Rhiannon Rasmussen-Silverstein
PRODUCTION MANAGER: Lissa Pattillo
MANAGING EDITOR: Julie Davis
ASSOCIATE PUBLISHER: Adam Arnold
PUBLISHER: Jason DeAngelis

ISBN: 978-1-64827-365-0
Printed in Canada
First Printing: November 2021
10 9 8 7 6 5 4 3 2 1

Adachi and Shimamura

NOVEL

7

STORY BY
Hitoma Iruma

ILLUSTRATED BY
Non

Airship

Seven Seas Entertainment

interlude What If...They Didn't Meet in the Gym Loft?

THE DAY I started taking the train was the first day it felt like I'd truly grown up. Not that I *felt more mature* or anything as impressive as that; I could just feel myself moving up the escalator to adulthood against my will. Mental growth wasn't easily measured, so the only real benchmark was age. The world saw me as an adult, and I was required to behave accordingly. Nothing more.

I took the train to the neighboring prefecture, then joined the flow of the crowd and walked to the subway entrance. I didn't have time to admire the glamorous golden clock that so often served as a meetup spot. Instead, I headed straight down the stairs, where the smell of people grew stronger—mostly perfume and hairspray. Down here, the noise offered me no peace.

From there, I took the subway to the next station, where I walked up and down yet more stairs to make yet another transfer. It wasn't far, but I sighed nonetheless. The dust seemed to cling to my skin, weighing me down.

Ever since I graduated and got a job, there was always a lingering sense of fatigue in the back of my mind that never went away.

As I stood on the platform waiting for the next train, my gaze wandered, and I spotted a woman standing three away with a lethargic look on her face. *We meet again,* I thought to myself. Her hair fell nearly to her waist, with a smattering of brown highlights that suggested she had bleached it quite some time ago, but it was her eyes that left an impression—deep mahogany and perpetually drowsy. She seemed like she was my age, and her schedule often overlapped with mine...but of course, she was still just a stranger. I didn't know her name. I'd never even *spoken* to her.

Then again, I didn't know a single other person here. Every day, we all boarded a train full of strangers and rode it to our distant destination. The longer I thought about it, the more it felt like a prison with no bars...or was it just because we were too far down to see the sky?

Then the train rolled into the station, and Ms. Sleepy and I boarded two different train cars. I was ever so faintly hoping I might score an empty seat today, but they all filled up in a blink. With a sigh, I leaned myself against the closed train doors on the opposite side of the car. Then I pressed my head against the window and sighed again. The day hadn't even started yet and I was already exhausted. Was this how it felt for everyone?

Desperate for a shred of motivation, I checked the date on my phone, but sure enough, it was only Thursday. Still another workday after this one. With no silver lining to keep me upright, my head slumped even farther.

Then, at last, the train started to move through the darkness, carrying me off to my own personal hell.

At my age, I had spent the majority of my life attending school, so perhaps that would explain why I was a student again in so many of my dreams—including the one from last night.

For some reason, we were all at school in the middle of the night, and the teachers were making us study, like some kind of detention all-nighter. It was awful. I found myself wishing I could go home and sleep, but then I realized: nothing was stopping me from doing just that. In a blink, I packed up my stuff and left the classroom (which was on the first floor and also the size of the entire gym for some reason). Then I jogged off into the night, breathing in the crisp air, and no one tried to stop me.

No surprise there, of course. After all, I wasn't a student anymore.

Right when this realization sank in, my alarm clock started ringing, and as my mind stirred awake, my real job filtered into the dream. Kinda funny.

I was always so *sleepy*. No matter how much sleep I got, the drowsiness lingered behind my eyeballs. But since I couldn't feel any fatigue anywhere else, evidently my body was getting enough rest. As I glared down at the villain who woke me, I slowly pushed myself up and started getting ready. While students had the luxury of skipping class if they felt like it, I wasn't so lucky. The dream was only a dream.

Before she left for school, my bratty sister told me to get my act together. Then my mother came in and shouted at me to quit dragging my feet. In that sense, nothing much had changed.

Once I washed my face, I started to feel a little more awake. In the mirror, I could see my own lifeless reflection. *No color,* I thought to myself as I touched my cheek. My skin was moisturized, but it still seemed pallid. *At least this way, I fit in with the rest of my coworkers,* I thought to myself with a dry laugh, averting my eyes.

I took a bus to the train station, then caught the train to the subway. I was starting to regret accepting a job so far away from home. Thus far, I had made all my decisions on a whim, and only now could I see my own mistakes. *That's life, I guess.* Biting back a yawn, I lined up and waited to board the train.

Just then, I noticed a familiar face. For whatever reason—maybe we both had the same schedule, or maybe she lived in my neighborhood—I saw a lot of this girl. She was hunched over slightly, her dark hair hanging like a veil of gloom over her eyes. She looked to be my age, though she was slightly taller. Other than that, she was a stranger.

Another yawn crept up on me, bringing tears to my eyes. I wiped them away and faced forward. The train would be here soon. Then it would take me to my destination, where I would spend eight miserable hours wishing I could leave.

Sure enough, the train arrived, and Miss Gloomy and I boarded two different train cars. There was an empty seat, but I chose not to take it. If I sat down, chances were high that I'd fall asleep and miss my stop, so I could only afford to sit on the evening train. But of course, the evening train was even *more* packed, so I rarely ever got a seat.

Instead, I walked to the pole grip near the seats and held onto it while my mind wandered. If I wasn't careful, I was in danger of falling asleep standing upright. So as the train paused at each station along the way, I looked up at the route map and thought to myself: Was the rest of my life going to be this boring? Would anything ever rock this boat?

I wasn't going to dive into the water unless there was something worth diving for. So if the ocean floor was empty, then all I wanted was to spend the rest of my time sleeping. That way I could minimize my suffering.

People often told me I was boring. Sometimes they were joking, and other times they really, really weren't. Either way, I never argued. Even I could see how boring my life was. And if my life was boring, then surely *I* was boring, too.

I spent every day going from my house to my job and back, with no real interest in anything and a tightly sealed lid on my numbed emotions. But I was used to it. It was exhausting and a total drag, but I could tolerate it.

When I thought about it, it wasn't much different from my time as a student. No close friends, no one to care about... The feeling was suffocating, like trying to talk with a parched throat. But the days ahead would offer no release from this misery. As long as I kept that in mind, I could endure it.

After I finished my mind-numbing work, I arrived at the subway station and headed down the stairs. Whenever I was on my way home, my sighs of exasperation turned into sighs of relief. Then the train arrived, and I shuffled on board, all the while listening to the frenzied footsteps of students racing down the stairs.

I walked quickly, straight to the vacant seat locked in my sights. Today, I wasn't letting anyone else take it. With a heavy sigh, I filled the vacancy...and right at the same moment, as if in perfect sync, someone else sat down beside me.

I looked over and froze, hovering halfway over the seat. It was the sleepy woman from this morning, sitting right next to me. Crouching forward, she looked back at me;

apparently, she recognized me as one of the familiar faces on her commute.

We gazed at each other, each of us recoiling slightly to make room for the other. Then the train started moving, and she grinned bashfully. Unlike her usual soporific stare, her gentle smile tickled my skin. I shook my head politely, then faced forward.

For the first time in a long time, something had breathed life into my numbed senses. Why did I feel so self-conscious? I kept glancing at her out of the corner of my eye. She was looking at me, too; her big, soft eyes peered at me curiously. Then our eyes met, and I felt my cheeks burn. Hastily, I faced forward once more.

I could feel the heat melting off all those layers of dust.

Why, though? We were just two strangers who took the same train, now sitting next to each other in the same train car. We still had yet to exchange a single word between us. So why was my heart racing so fast? My usual slumped posture was now suddenly as straight as a pin.

I knew how far I was going; the same could be said for her. We didn't have anything to talk about. We were just sitting together... *Together*? Did it really count as "sitting together"? We sat down next to each other purely by chance. It was a coincidence at best.

But then again, maybe that was just how it worked. Nobody *decided* we would meet one day, but for some reason, our lives intersected at this one tiny point. Maybe I didn't control these things as much as I thought I did.

The train slowed to a stop. Soon this moment would come to an end. So before I missed my chance altogether, I offered her my interest.

"Hey, um...what's your name?"

Even if we had missed the chance to meet somewhere before, destiny had brought us together again. And it was that single destiny that flipped the whole script.

I had a dream. It was so awesome, I couldn't even remember what happened. But whatever it was, it was *awesome*.

1. Smile, Smile, Shining Bright

I COULD HEAR some kind of clapping sound, but it wasn't my hands. My curtains were closed, and yet I could already see light shining in through my window. In a blink, it had gone from night to morning...and my body felt as light as a feather. Granted, I didn't generally have trouble waking up in the morning, but why did I feel so *good*?

I flung open the curtains—and what I saw took my breath away.

The rising sun had lit up the rooftops and trees, softening all the sharp edges with the warm, fuzzy glow of morning. Never before had the sunlight looked so magical. All it took was a little change of mindset to change the whole world... Wait, no. My mindset *was* my whole world.

These were things I'd read in a book somewhere, but only now did it all finally click.

When I hopped out of bed, it felt like I was walking on clouds—springy like a trampoline, but not stable. I could scarcely feel the carpet beneath my toes. I paced around and around the room, my mind unfocused, unable to think of an objective. *What do I do first?* I kept wandering to and fro, distracted by every possibility I came across. It felt like my brain might shut down altogether if I wasn't careful.

Eventually I sat down in the center of my room and pulled out a dictionary.

"C... Co... Cou..."

I sounded like a pigeon.

Couple: two people who are married, engaged, or otherwise romantically involved.

Dating: two people in an intimate relationship.

Girlfriend: a regular female companion with whom a person has a romantic relationship.

I slammed the book shut and flopped to the floor. My chest ached so bad, I couldn't breathe. My solar plexus felt tight, and my limbs felt heavy from the lack of oxygen. I knew I needed to fill my lungs, but when I opened my mouth, the air clogged my throat in a single mass that suffocated me even more. I buried my face in the carpet and coughed.

After I writhed for a while, I rolled onto my back and clutched my chest. My skin was burning hotter and hotter like it was cooking in the summer sun. Then my neck flushed pink, and my heart started to race, bringing with it nausea and a headache. Still, I didn't really mind it. In a way, it was refreshing. All these different maladies were bringing me to life.

As my mind swirled like a merry-go-round, I finally regained a tiny piece of composure: *Okay, let's just calm down for a minute.* Why was I freaking out? I wasn't sweaty when I woke up, so why was my shirt soaked? As I took a deep breath, I ran my fingers through my thoroughly warmed hair and retraced my steps as calmly as possible.

Right now, it's morning...and before, it was last night... Ugh, I'm already not making any sense! I scratched my head. *Last night...I went to a festival with Shimamura, and, uh...now it's the next day.*

Only ten hours had passed since then, and yet the memories felt as distant as fireworks in the night sky. The details were so fuzzy, I was starting to worry it was all just a dream. I didn't even remember *how I got home* last night.

Everything that happened after Shimamura said yes was a blur—much like the way I could only ever remember the good parts of my dreams. I seemed to recall her taking my hand and leading me home, and I was pretty sure we talked about something, but I couldn't remember what she said to me or how I responded. Normally, I remembered *everything* about Shimamura, so I must have been in pretty bad shape.

Yes, it was a mind-blowing night. First, I told Shimamura that I loved her. She asked me what I wanted from her. Then one thing led to another, and we decided to be girlfriends.

I clapped my hands to my cheeks. I was too restless to sit still; my toes were wiggling like they had half a mind to take off without me. Frankly, anyone in my shoes who could stay calm was probably a psychopath. The whole room was spinning.

Being Shimamura's girlfriend was probably—*definitely*—proof that I was special. That was what meant the most to me. We were vitally important and irreplaceable to each other...right? Immediately, I started to question myself. For some reason I felt vaguely uneasy, like maybe I was still dreaming. The sun had risen on a new day, just like always, and I was functionally awake, but my mind was still drunk on those festival lantern lights.

So I asked myself: *What do I do now?* I could hear my bones rattling in my body, and it took me a few minutes before I found the otherwise extremely obvious answer: *Just take it one problem at a time. First, let's make sure it wasn't a dream.*

I picked up my phone, opened my nearly empty address book, and pulled up Shimamura's entry. The mere sight of her name made my palms sweaty. Then the fear and excitement set in all at once, wrestling for dominance until my stomach hurt. If only I had the good sense to wait until those feelings faded, perhaps I could save myself a little embarrassment on a daily basis—but of course, I never had time for that.

It took a while for Shimamura to answer, but then she finally picked up.

"...Nnhello?"

Her voice had all the energy of a wet paper towel. Instinctively, I straightened up—and gave myself a cramp in the process. Then my confidence faltered, and I shrank back down again. "Hey, um...good morning." My throat was already on fire.

"Oh, hi, Adachi... What's up?"

She still sounded half-asleep. I knew she wasn't an early bird, but really? Then I looked up at the clock and realized it was only 6 a.m. Anybody would be sleepy! Now I was starting to feel bad for calling her without thinking it through. A cold sweat trickled down my back. "Sorry, um... You were sleeping, huh?"

"Mmhm... 'm sleepy..."

Her responses were getting weaker by the second. If I waited too long, chances were good she'd fall asleep on me. "Should I...call you back later? I should, shouldn't I?"

"No, it's okay... Did you need something?"

She sounded like the same old Shimamura. And I was the same old me—panicking and stumbling like always. *Wait, what? So...nothing's changed?* This realization calmed me down a bit. I just needed to try my best, like normal. *Frankly, it's a miracle I made it this far with no chill whatsoever.*

"Listen, um..."

"Yeah?"

I had so many questions I wanted to ask: *How did I get home last night? Did I have a mental breakdown? Was I even conscious?* But at their root, they all led to the most important question of all, so I decided to lead with that.

Swallowing, I gripped the phone. If it turned out the whole thing was a dream, I was about to humiliate myself on a "lifelong trauma" type of level. It was tantamount to walking off a cliff.

"You and me are...d...day...ting now...right?" I asked, my voice cracking. Then I started to hiccup, too. *Lifelong trauma, here I come!*

"Uhhh... I think so."

How can you be so casual about this?! Reflexively, I flailed my legs against the floor. "So...um...l-last night..."

"Yup, as of last night," she replied, as airily as a party balloon.

It wasn't a dream. Everything that happened yesterday had now led to today. I bowed my head, giving thanks to my past self for every little step she took to bring me here. "Well, I...I'm looking forward to it."

"Uh huh. Me too." I could hear her hair rustling on the other end of the line.

Maybe it was too much to ask, since she was so sleepy, but...I was...kind of hoping she'd be a bit more excited than that... *No, if I want something, then I need to put myself out there and get it!*

"I...I really love you, so...um..." I couldn't think of a smart way to lead into it, so instead I just said it flat-out.

Times like these, it was painfully apparent just how inexperienced I was. But I only had myself to blame.

"Oh, wow... Gosh... Thanks."

Her long, drawn-out pauses made me blush all the way to my ears. Then the conversation died. As usual, I had no clue what else I was supposed to say. Instead, I suffocated in the heat and silence.

"Well, um...guess I'll go," I stammered.

"Okay."

"Um...sleep well?" This was not something I usually said at 6 a.m.

"I will indeed..."

I could hear her voice pulling away. Our relationship had changed, and yet neither of us were any different over the phone. Was this normal? I couldn't be sure.

But just then...her breath returned to my ear.

"I love you too."

And then she hung up.

"......What?"

WHAT?!

A sprinkling of warm droplets beaded all over my face. I could feel a hole in my chest like my soul had been dislodged; meanwhile, my neck felt like it was overstuffed. Slowly but surely, this feeling permeated my entire body.

Then I leapt up, crawling around the floor on my elbows and knees, clutching my burning face and writhing in shame as the words replayed over and over in my head. It felt like I'd swallowed something toxic, and I was in no condition to think straight. Instead, I pressed my fingers to my eyes and quietly endured it.

But I quickly hit my breaking point.

God, she—she just—ADSDHGKLGSDK!!!

"Whaddafaaa... whaaaddaFAAAA! BWAAAHH! Buh-buh-buh-buh-buh!"

I flailed my limbs like a dying housefly.

On that mid-August morning, the cicadas' drone started to wane...and a different creature howled in their place. This marked the start of many dreamy days to come.

When I next awoke, clutching my head, I wondered if maybe the phone conversation was all a dream too. Whenever good things happened to me, it made me nervous, because I knew real life wasn't like that. Real life was unforgiving.

But on second thought, maybe I was a little bit off there. Maybe real life wasn't *unforgiving*—just apathetic to our individual struggles. Real life was everything that surrounded us: the environment we lived in, the air we breathed, our interpersonal relationships, and all the furthest reaches of the galaxy... When I stopped to think about it, none of these were directly connected to one single person.

Thus, real life had no interest in us. It didn't pick on us, nor did it help us; things simply *happened*, and whether every roll of the dice was a 6 or a 1, no one was behind the wheel. There was no need to tremble in fear, waiting for the other shoe to drop. But of course, conversely, it meant nothing would save me from a string of unlucky events either.

"But...!"

I sat cross-legged on the floor and swayed from side to side. No amount of philosophical pondering was going to allay my short-term worries. Should I call her back at lunchtime and ask her to confirm what she said? I smacked my forehead and my hair. Why did I always lash out at myself whenever I was feeling ashamed?

And another thing: why was I always such a...such a *wet noodle* whenever I talked to Shimamura? I used to be able to speak my mind, so what happened? I tucked my knees under my chin and mulled it over. If growing up had somehow made me less capable than I was before, then I wasn't growing up the right way—or so a wise person once said. Then again, I wasn't exactly the most capable kid either.

I'm just desperate for Shimamura to love me, I thought with a sigh. That was why I spent so much time carefully choosing my words, whereas in the past I spoke freely and without fear. Looking back, I used to be a pretty decent communicator. *Well, should I try to speak with no filter?* I asked myself, like an idiot. Then my brain answered: *That's just not possible. She's the one person I don't want to hurt.*

Relationships were so complicated. Especially when you were emotionally invested.

I nuzzled my face against my knees and zoned out. I had been granted my heart's deepest desire, and now I was feeling it out, trying to find the line between dream and reality. Once it all hit home, though, I'd probably start running around like a chicken with its head cut off. *Seriously, can't I just keep it together for once?*

Then I started thinking: If I could have stayed the way I was before, would my relationship with Shimamura be any different? More open, maybe? Less...stagnant? There was so much I couldn't control about myself... but then again, maybe that was part of the human experience.

I sighed. For some reason, I really wanted to hear her voice again. I could feel my eardrums yearning for her. *Should I call her?* I reached out to grab my phone. *Oh, but I could always go see her in person. I could go to her house, and...*

"...Nah, that's okay."

I decided not to meet up with her in person just yet. There was no telling how I might embarrass myself this time, and I didn't want her to change her mind about me. Instead, I needed to give myself some extra time to calm down and organize my thoughts first. In fact, maybe it could wait until the start of the new semester.

Still, a quick call wouldn't hurt, I thought to myself as my outstretched hand finally settled on my cell phone. I just needed to take it one step at a time and answer each question as it came to me.

This time she answered quickly.

"Uh, Shimamura?"

"Morning!" She sounded much more awake—and much more her usual self.

The instant her voice reached my ears, I remembered the last thing she said before, and my cheeks tingled. "Hey, good morning... You awake?"

She laughed. "Well, duh. What time do you think it is?"

I looked up at the clock: 10 a.m. She made it sound like she wouldn't normally be asleep right about now, but frankly, I could easily picture her sleeping in until noon.

"So what's up?" she asked.

"Uhhh..."

I decided to skip the small talk and cut right to the chase. The longer I talked, the more likely I was to put my foot in my mouth.

"Earlier, um..." I could feel my heart throbbing in my throat. "Th-the whole 'I love you' thing..."

"Oh, yeah, that. You said that already, but thank you."

"No, uh, that's not what I meant..."

"So you didn't mean it? Wow. I'm devastated."

"Wha... No, I... No, no, no! I mean *you*, not me!"

"What about me?"

"You...you told me you love me...right?"

Somehow, she thought I was talking about when *I* said it to *her*, not the other way around. I hunched myself up in a tight little ball and endured the burning shame.

"...Did I?"

"What?"

I got the sense maybe she was teasing me to distract from her own embarrassment. *Ha ha, very funny.* But then the silence lingered, and I realized she was serious. My jokey response evaporated into thin air before I could say a word of it.

"Umm...Adachi? Are you mad at me?"

"Urgh..." I swallowed hard. "No, uh...I mean, not really..."

"Aha! So you admit you're mad at me! Look, I'm sorry—I honestly don't remember."

I tried to deny it, but she saw right through me. Still, what I felt wasn't really *anger*; I was just on the verge of becoming an emotional wreck. But for Shimamura, it was probably easier to sum it up by saying I was mad instead. Honestly, she wasn't far off, and the fact that she could make these split-second judgments was proof of her vastly superior social skills. In her shoes, I would have hesitated and stammered.

"Really, though...I'm not *mad*, but..."

"But?"

Naturally, she was quick to notice that I had more to say too. *She actually really understands me!* The thought made me light up with joy. But I couldn't just sit there and sparkle, of course.

"I...I want you to...say it again," I stammered. To my own ears, it was asking far too much. But if she didn't remember, then we could always just do it over again. Well, okay, maybe not *always*. But in this case, there was still time.

"Wha? Come on... Gimme a break..." Her voice shifted, suggesting she'd moved her head. "It's a little embarrassing...and by a little, I mean a lot..."

"Just...just try!"

"I don't think it's that easy..."

In my excitement, I sat up straight, waiting eagerly. This was possibly the first time I'd ever asked someone to tell me they loved me...or at least, I couldn't remember ever asking my parents. Maybe that was why the impact of it swatted me like a fly the first time around. But as far as I was concerned, Shimamura was allowed to swat me anytime.

I was so worked up, I could feel myself starting to breathe more heavily. But I didn't want to sound like a creep over the phone, so I exhaled slowly, suppressing my panic. Then I held my breath.

"I love you, Adachi."

Her voice was just as warm as last time. If I was a water heater, steam would be gushing from my ears right now. *Wait, does the "water heater" part even matter? Ugh, I don't know!* All I knew for sure was that I was melting on the inside.

"In fact, I love you sooo much, the words slipped out subconsciously...I guess."

"Wh-what part?" I asked, for personal reference.

"What?"

"What's your favorite thing about me?" I clarified. Then I heard her pause.

"Ummm...I love that you *don't* ask me those kinds of questions! Ha ha..."

I thought about it, but I was still confused. "I don't get it."

"No luck, huh? Was kinda hoping I could get out of answering..."

This caught my attention. "So you don't have a favorite thing about me?"

"Sure I do! Lots! But when you put me on the spot, I need a minute to think of the answer, that's all."

"You do...?"

She sure didn't seem to "need a minute" to tell me about her chocolate preferences. If it was so hard to answer the question, then did she really even love me at all?

"What about you, Adachi? Can *you* name the things you love about *me*?"

"Yup. I can think of all kinds of things." *Enough to fill a whole notebook, in fact. Because I literally filled a whole notebook.*

"Whoa... That's really surprising."

"What? No, it isn't." *A few conversations were all it took to make me dream of kissing you, Shimamura. You're just that great.*

"All kinds of things? Really?"

"Really. Tons of stuff."

I could speak more confidently about Shimamura than I could about myself. It was obvious which of us I cared about more.

"Well, okay. That's good." She sounded pretty convinced. "You know, I think there's value in asking other people to point out the things you can't see for yourself."

Evidently, the concept resonated with her somehow... but it didn't seem like she was going to clue me in, and the distance between us frustrated me.

"And now that we're together, you'll teach me what my good points are, right?"

Despite my impatience, I could sense that she was still willing to make things work, and that alone was enough to set my heart aflame. "I...I'll do my best!" I agreed eagerly, balling my hands into fists. *I'll always be right there for you.*

"Hee hee! Okay, I look forward to it."

"Uh...c-cool!"

I'm gonna point out tons of stuff. Trust me, you won't be disappointed.

Later, after that phone call came to an end, my brain felt floaty—similar to the detachment of anxiety, but with soft, fuzzy edges. Then it hit me: *Wait, but she didn't answer the question I asked her!* I wasn't mad, though. If anything, I was continually impressed by her conversational skills.

"Hee hee hee hee hee..."

I could hear a creepy laugh coming from somewhere.

Then I looked around the room and realized: it was *my* creepy laugh.

Naturally, I started laughing harder.

I was sitting in the corner of the room, knees tucked under my chin. Couldn't begin to pinpoint where I was or what time it was. After all, the majority of my life was spent this way.

Since childhood, I was notoriously terrible at making friends. The other kids were all just as inexperienced as I was, and yet they seemed to have a natural sense for social situations in a way that I simply didn't. Why? Was I born with a defective soul? Did humans even have souls to begin with? If so, then where did they come from?

If I inherited it from my parents, could I blame all my problems on them? No, of course I couldn't. I was the one in control; I was free to decide for myself what constituted as friendship. But instead, I just sat there in the corner and did nothing. That was how I lived my life...until now. Now I ventured out into the light of day, beneath the rising sun.

Today was September 1st: the first day of the new school semester.

A year ago, I didn't even attend the entrance ceremony. I was fickle and lazy; I didn't go to class, so I fell behind. But it wasn't a waste of time, and I didn't regret it. After all, that was how I met Shimamura. That alone was enough to light up my world.

To me, September 1st marked the start of a new year with Shimamura by my side.

I grabbed my bicycle and set off in the opposite direction of the school. It was still early, and the sun wasn't quite up, but I didn't need it. Soon, I would be with Shimamura. And to me, her smile shone brighter than any star.

interlude

What If... Adachi Had Stayed Aloof?

A S ALWAYS, Adachi was up in the gym loft...and as always, I was up there visiting her. The weather was cooling down, and as the sun set a little earlier with each passing day, I could feel the world transitioning into autumn. Even the cicadas had fallen quiet.

"Oh." She heard me coming and looked up at me as she idly toyed with her cell phone. "Hey."

She raised her hand in a quick wave, and I waved back. Then I set my bag down on the ping-pong table and sat down near her...or maybe beside her? *Yeah, "beside her" has a nice ring to it,* I nodded to myself. Then I uncapped the mineral water I bought on my way here and took a sip.

"Ugh, lucky. Can I have some?"

She held out her palm, and I set the bottle on it. "Thanks."

Then she started chugging—no consideration given to the fact that it was someone else's drink. Not that I really minded all that much. Instead, I sat there and took it all in: the clear water, the plastic bottle, and Adachi herself. Her tidy hair, her slender neck... It was all so *picturesque*.

It was a weekday, and school was in session. Nevertheless, here we were. This was our normal routine. I still went to class every now and then, but Adachi never joined me; she was a true dyed-in-the-wool delinquent. Not that this was something to be proud of, of course.

What did she do on the days I wasn't around? I tried asking her, but she responded with a vague "Eh, I just do whatever." To me, this was not a satisfying answer.

"Thanks," she repeated as she handed the bottle back to me. As I rolled it around in my hands, I could feel her lingering warmth on the plastic, quickly overwritten by my own. Next, I held up the bottle and gazed at the gym wall through the lens of the water—but this did nothing to make the room sparkle. It was as dull as my own plain eyesight.

I lowered my arm and looked back at Adachi, who was currently zoning out. She wasn't stiff, but she wasn't relaxed, either; her body language was shaped by her sheer lack of interest in anything around her. She would stay in this mode until I spoke to her.

Honestly, the fact that I knew all this was proof that I'd been paying attention to her. But the longer I thought about it, the sweatier my palms became. *Weird.*

"Hey," I called. She turned to face me, and once again I found myself admiring her long bangs. "What do you like to do when you're by yourself?"

I had already asked her this same question in the past, but I felt like trying again. Like last time, she frowned faintly and cocked her head. "I dunno... Stuff?"

Nothing worth explaining, apparently. *Well, okay, then.* All I could really do was try to see for myself.

"Okay, Adachi, go wander around alone somewhere."

"What?"

"I'll follow at a distance."

She blinked, confounded. Her eyes darted to and fro as she tried to parse it. Then she fixed me with a funny look. "What are you *talking* about?"

"Well, I want to see what you get up to. Surveillance!" I explained, cupping my hands around my eyes like binoculars.

She leaned in, peering past my hands, and for a moment we gazed at each other—a moment in which I desperately tried to pretend I didn't look like a total idiot.

"You want me to act like you're not there...even though you are?"

"Yeah, exactly."

"What? Isn't that gonna be kinda hard?"

"Well...maybe?" I clapped her on the shoulder. "Just try your best!"

"Uggghhh..." At first she narrowed her eyes in annoyance, but after I sat there waiting hopefully for long enough, she grabbed her bookbag and rose to her feet.

"That's the spirit!" I exclaimed gleefully as I followed after her.

Together, we left the gym, moving along the outer building wall to avoid detection by any teachers as we made our way to the front gates. Once we ran out of shadows to hide in, I craned my head back and stared straight up.

"Wow..."

The wind wailed in my ears as it shuttled the puffy white clouds. *Now that's a fine blue sky,* I thought to myself, quoting a manga I once read. This same quote had stuck with me for years now. Days like these, I wished I could watch the sky while I walked, but today, I was supposed to be watching Adachi.

I fixed my eyes on her as I maintained a careful distance.

Her posture could use some work... On second thought, she's walking way too fast. If she's gonna be a delinquent, she needs to have more swagger! That said, she looked right at home walking off campus in the middle of the day.

Just then, she looked over her shoulder at me. I waved at her; she waved back slightly, then faced forward and started trudging along. *Wait, but...didn't you take your bike to school today?*

She was supposed to ignore me, but she kept glancing back and making eye contact with me. Maybe it was unreasonable to expect her to pretend I wasn't here. After it happened a few more times, she came to a complete stop and waited for me to catch up.

"Ugh, I can't. I give up."

"Aww, c'mon!"

"Okay, well, why don't we just walk *together*?" she suggested, eyes averted, indicating the space next to her.

Oh, Adachi, how do you manage to be so adorable? I looked up at the sky and thought for a moment, debating which I'd prefer.

"Sure, let's do that." And so I forfeited my surveillance post and stepped right up next to her. Together, we headed into the city.

Well, what now? My heart pounded in time with the

dotted white lines on the road.

"It's just...boring."

"What?"

She kept her eyes on the street ahead. "Walking alone, zoning out... It's boring."

That much I could see for myself just by looking at her face, but a beat later, I realized: she was answering my question about how she spent her alone time. Evidently, she had figured out how to explain it to me.

"That's all I can really say about it," she shrugged, though her eyes silently asked me if it was enough. I nodded—but who gave *me* the right to decide that, anyway? I was all too giddy.

"Gotcha..."

For once, Adachi had revealed a tiny part of her inner self, like a drop of water trickling out from behind the ice. Shivering in the light autumn chill, I gladly accepted her for who she was, and I was eager to embark on this journey with her. Or would she find it boring, walking downtown with me? Her indifferent expression didn't reveal much, so I'd just have to ask her at some point.

The next day, we were back up in the gym loft. It was our hideout—the one place we could relax and be ourselves.

The word *sanctuary* came to mind… Then I chuckled to myself.

Now I'm just being dramatic.

I had a dream where I was riding on top of a giant Yashiro-zilla, soaring through the stars. It was fun.

I could feel myself grinning like an idiot. Honestly, if it happened in real life, I'd probably be scared witless. Good thing some dreams don't come true.

2. A moment's Respite

IT WAS THE MORNING of the entrance ceremony: the end of summer vacation and the start of lethargic depression.

I awoke from the heat but stubbornly lingered under the covers. Starting today, I would have to wake up at a certain time every morning, get dressed, and leave the house early enough to arrive in time for first period. This was going to be impossible for someone like me, whose muscles had atrophied over summer break. Drowsiness and laziness leaked from every pore, engulfing me. My eyelids were so heavy, they practically vacuum-sealed my eyes shut.

Then I noticed I couldn't hear any cicadas crying through the window behind me. Summer was ending, each moment of it repurposed as a memory of a time long since passed, in order to make room for autumn. I could never go back to the past, nor could I remain here in the present. I had no choice but to flow with the seasons ever onward.

In other words, if I kept snoozing, maybe I'd end up in the same place regardless... *Yeah, probably... Zzzzz...*

"Geddup!"

Out of nowhere, someone kicked me in the butt. I rolled away with the blanket, but the foot chased after me.

"Take that! Take that!"

Are you having fun kicking your own daughter's butt, Mom?

Once I hit the wall, I had no choice but to wake up. She grinned at me, flashing her pearly whites. "Good morning."

I looked over at my little sister, a notorious early bird, but she was still sound asleep in bed. "Uh...what time is it?"

My organs groaned as my internal clock hitched. This was clearly not enough sleep for me. But my mother didn't answer; instead, her eyes narrowed into slits. "Your friend's outside."

"*Friend*? What friend?" I asked, shaking my sleepy head. But once again, no answer came, and she left the room.

If they came to my house, then it's Adachi or Tarumi... and since it's the first day of school...probably Adachi. I'm gonna laugh if it's Nagafuji, though.

I opened the curtains and peeked outside. "Aha."

Sure enough, I could see Adachi standing out in front of my house, her forehead glistening with sweat beneath the first rays of the morning sun. Why was she hunching her shoulders like that? She was standing there all stiff like a robot, face and neck flushed bright red, unmoving. Idly, I wondered if she was holding her breath.

"Hmmm...I guess she's waiting for me...?"

Of course she is. I stepped away from the window. Honestly, I would have liked to observe her in Robot Mode a little longer, but if she really was holding her breath, then I didn't want her to suffocate. Thus, I decided to go fetch her.

I left my room without bothering to get dressed or brush my hair. Come to think of it, despite all our phone calls, I hadn't seen Adachi in person in quite a while— not since the summer festival, in fact. I kept expecting her to show up at my house, but she never did. Maybe she needed to sort out her feelings...or maybe not.

While we're on the subject, that festival night was hell on earth. Adachi turned into a soulless husk, so I had to practically carry her back home, and it was *sweltering*. Kinda made me wish she would've waited to confess her feelings until we got to her house... Selfish, I know. This was one of the things I probably needed to change about myself.

My mind reviewed all of the night's events in order, and by the end, I was blushing faintly. "Eeee...!"

This was my first experience having a girlfriend...but then again, that was probably normal, since plenty of girls went their whole lives without ever having one. Or was it actually pretty common, and I just didn't know about it? Like Hino and Nagafuji, for example. They seemed really close, so maybe something was going on there...

Meh, who cares. More importantly, I needed to figure out what to say when I opened the door. Our relationship had evolved from "friends" to "girlfriends," so what else was going to change? Was I supposed to be different somehow? When she asked me out, I said yes under the assumption that Future Me would figure it all out...and now I *was* Future Me.

"Help me, Doraemon..."

I had finished all my homework, but there was just one big problem left. The same problem I'd procrastinated on.

Normally, girls didn't get girlfriends—you know, generally speaking. But Adachi was different...and the fact that I agreed to date her probably meant I was too...

"*Eeeeeee...!*"

Unfortunately, the thirty seconds it took to arrive at the front door was nowhere near enough time for my sleepy brain to figure something out. In the end, I decided I would just act normal.

When I opened the door, I found she was still in Robot Mode. "Good morning," I greeted her. She flinched in fear, eyes quavering in contrast with her otherwise perfect stillness. Since she was wearing her uniform, she was probably here to take me to school.

This year, she wasn't planning to hide out in the gym loft. Plus, my hair was a different color, and now I wouldn't have to walk to school alone. The days that came before all blurred together, and yet they had brought about a dozen tiny changes that added up to today. At last, I had arrived at the second semester of my second year of high school, and the only thing that had stayed the same was the miserable heat.

Then Adachi started toddling over to me, her shoulders still hunched. Her joints were so stiff, she looked like she was bunny-hopping.

"Hmmmm." *She reminds me of a bouncy ball. Boing, boing, boing. Looks like fun.* Anyone would smile if they saw her, and I was no exception.

Then, with a *whoosh*, she landed right in front of me. *She sure knows how to make an entrance, I guess.* She still hadn't said a single word, and yet her lower lip was now quivering along with her eyes. I was relieved to see she was the same girl I remembered—but just then, she whipped her head down into a deep bow.

"I...I'm really looking forward to this!"

I could practically hear her stiff joints creaking as she straightened up again. What was she even talking about? I paused to think.

"Ohhhh, I get it."

She was talking about our new relationship. It kinda felt like today was officially our first day together... The thought made me a little bashful.

"Well, um, I am too."

I bowed back to her. After all, I got the sense I was more exasperating to her than she was to me. Plus, I didn't know how to date anyone. I thought back to the disclaimer I once muttered under my breath: *Don't blame me if it doesn't work out.* Looking back, maybe this was the moment I should have said it for real.

"So...what are you doing here at the crack of dawn?"

She recoiled sharply. "I...I thought maybe we could...go to school together..."

"Oh ho." Clearly she was planning to turn me into an honor student.

"Because I...I mean, you're my...g-girl...girlfriend now..." She was so visibly nervous, her teeth were chattering.

"Uh..." Technically we were *both* girlfriends, so how did that work? *Eh, whatever.*

"Aren't you?" she pressed, taking a step forward, and I half-expected her to grab my hand. When she looked up, I realized our faces were inches apart.

She had asked me this same question over the phone. Was she really that insecure about it? Granted, she was practically unconscious for the latter half of that night, so maybe she just couldn't remember for sure. Maybe she thought she dreamed the whole thing. Therefore...

"Yes, I am."

It was a little embarrassing, but nevertheless, I took her hand in mine, lacing my fingers with hers with our palms pressed together. She flinched and looked at me like a deer in headlights. I slowly raised our joined hands for her to see.

"I love you, and you love me. Right?"

It's just that simple.

Slowly, she wilted. Or maybe she had simply switched out of Robot Mode. In exchange, her cheeks lit up scarlet.

"...Right."

Coming from her, this was actually a fairly confident response. Kind of anticlimactic, actually. Then I heard footsteps approaching from behind me and hastily pulled my hand away.

"Hello there!"

For some reason, my mother had decided to say hi to Adachi too. I gestured for her to get lost, but she grabbed me by the face and pushed me away.

"I see you're here pretty early. Did you eat breakfast?"

Talking to my mom always made Adachi tense...or maybe that was my fault.

"Oh, no, I never eat breakfast..."

"Well, then, that works out perfectly. Come on in and eat something."

"Huh?!"

Without waiting for her answer, my mother grabbed her by the arm and dragged her inside. "You come along too," she added, beckoning to me.

"Yes, Mom," I sighed. As the door swung shut, I glanced

outside one last time. "You know we have plenty of time still, right?"

Why is everyone in such a rush all the time?

I followed them into the kitchen. My sister was still asleep, but Yashiro was present and accounted for, eating a plate of cabbage piled high with miso sauce at the ready nearby. "What a wonderful morning!" she announced as we entered.

"Really now?" *I guess every morning's a "wonderful morning" when you get to waltz into someone else's house and eat their food free of charge.*

"Ah, if it isn't Shimamura-san and Adachi-san." She was like a cow vigorously chewing her cud, and yet her voice wasn't muffled at all. Almost like she didn't use her mouth to talk... Pretty suspicious if you asked me. But then again, everything about her was suspicious, so it didn't matter much.

"Good morning," I greeted her as I sat down in the chair next to her.

She offered me her plate. "Would you like some?"

"No, that's okay," I declined. She promptly went back to chomping her cabbage.

Of course, I knew full well that she'd help herself to a serving of *our* breakfast too. Maybe she had the metabolism of a little mouse, so she needed to eat something at all hours of the day. That being said, how on earth did she convince my mother to serve her *shredded cabbage* for breakfast? Not that I expected either of them to pay any mind to societal conventions, but still. It was a total mystery.

Adachi's gaze wandered around the table in search of a place to sit. "You can just sit there," I told her, gesturing to my father's usual spot. Like everyone else in my family, he was an early bird, so he was already at work.

Seriously, I keep trying to go to bed early... Where am I going wrong?

With her eyes locked on mine, Adachi slowly lowered herself into my father's chair, perching at the very edge like a total awkward nerd. Not that anyone here really minded.

"It seems we've got a full house this morning!" Yashiro exclaimed cheerfully.

"You can say that again. Ha ha ha!" my mother responded as she set plates down in front of us. "Today's a short day, so I figure you won't need more than toast."

"Okay," I nodded.

"Adachi-chan, which do you prefer: butter or strawberry jam?" my mother called from the fridge, holding up the two condiments in question.

Adachi looked from one to the other. "Oh, no, I... I mean, jam's fine."

She was totally going to decline both, but then decided it'd be rude and changed her answer. *Trust me, you don't have to worry about that.*

My mother pulled a slice of bread from the bag and put it on Adachi's plate, then set the jam jar down on the table nearby. "There you go."

"Th-thank you, ma'am," Adachi replied, avoiding eye contact. It was obvious she didn't have much experience interacting with *anyone's* mother, least of all mine. I could see her legs jiggling anxiously under the table; stiffly, she reached out and spread a paper-thin layer of jam onto the bread. *Oh, come on.*

"You can put as much as you want, you know. Like that," my mother told her, pointing at Yashiro, who was pouring miso sauce on her cabbage.

"Condiments make food taste better," Yashiro announced matter-of-factly, then started crunching like a cow again. *Eh, forget about her.*

Adachi picked up her toast and took a tiny bite, her eyes busily darting to and fro. Why was she eating breakfast with us anyway? It was so surreal—I was baffled. But of course, my mother didn't care one bit. She dropped a slice of bread onto my plate too, almost as an after-thought. "Here, eat up."

"Not gonna ask me if I want jam or butter?"

"Not like you care."

That's not true, you jerk!

I waffled for a moment, then settled on butter. Meanwhile, she sat at the table and watched Adachi eat. "Hmmm..."

Unsurprisingly, Adachi started to choke on her food like she'd forgotten how to swallow. Then it occurred to me that I'd never seen her actually *enjoy* anything she ate. She never had much of an appetite. Maybe that was why she didn't really seem *alive*, except in the literal sense. *How could I get her to eat with a smile...?*

My mother, meanwhile, was still acting like a total weirdo, crouching low against the table so she could get a look at Adachi's face from below. "Hmmmmmm..."

"Nnngh..."

"Uh, Mom, you're really bothering us right now," I snapped at her.

"Hah!"

She blew me off with a laugh. *Seriously, who does that?* I was both annoyed and impressed at the same time.

"So you came to pick up ol' Sleeping Beauty?"

"What did you just call me...?"

"Uh, yes, ma'am..."

Hello?! Don't just ignore me!

"Well, you sure showed up early. Were you that excited to see her?"

"Oh... Sorry, Shimamura. Did I wake you?" Her eyes drifted from my bedhead to my PJs as she donned a guilty frown.

"Meh, don't feel bad about her. She would sleep 24/7 if we let her."

"She was asking *me*, not you!"

By this point, I was too tired to argue. Not like my mother was going to listen... But just then, she smiled at me. "You've made a good friend for once."

"Yeah, I guess." *Except she's actually my girlfriend.*

If I actually said that part out loud, would she have a heart attack? Or would she be cool with it? I rolled my eyes at myself. *Ugh, who am I kidding? No way.*

Then I noticed Yashiro staring pointedly at my hands, a cabbage shred dangling from her lips. A beat later, I realized she was actually staring at my *toast*. It didn't take a rocket scientist to figure out what she wanted.

"Here."

I tore off a piece of buttered bread and offered it to her. Sure enough, she leaned in and chomped. *Am I crazy, or did she stretch her neck way farther than humanly possible? Eh, must've been seeing things.* After she devoured the bread, she offered me her veggies. "In return, you may help yourself to my cabbage."

"Pass."

She ignored me and sprinkled her miso cabbage directly onto the rest of my bread. Now it was...uh...miso butter cabbage toast. Or a miso cutlet sandwich, minus the cutlet. I didn't appreciate this, but decided to taste it anyway.

"Hmmm... Not that weird, I guess." But I also wasn't ten years old, so it wasn't the kind of thing I would choose to eat on purpose. "Huh?"

Just then, I noticed Adachi staring at me from behind her toast, her expression less than favorable, and I had a feeling I knew why.

"Trade you a bite?"

"Sure."

I could practically see the light bulb appear over her head. Evidently, I had guessed correctly. We each tore off a piece, then set it on the other's plate.

Nom nom. "Hm." I could barely taste the jam at all.

After we ate, there was still some time before we needed to leave. But my kid sister was asleep in our bedroom, so I left Yashiro the mouse to the rest of her cabbage and led Adachi upstairs.

"Sorry, but it's gonna be hot up here."

She nodded in understanding, her ears as pink as the thin layer of strawberry jam. But she seemed nervous for some reason, and I was mildly concerned she might switch back to Robot Mode. If only her social skills were as developed as her gross motor skills.

We walked into the study room, and Adachi promptly knelt down on the floor, her pointer finger restlessly tracing her knee. Now she looked like a little kid who got caught misbehaving. *Oh, what am I gonna do with you?* To combat the heat, I pulled out the electric fan and switched it on.

Just then, she bowed to me deeply. "I...I'm looking forward to this!"

I nearly bowed back, but caught myself. "We already did this part earlier."

"Well, we have to do it again!"

She sounded so insistent, I ended up buying into it. "Uhh...okay...?" *I guess these formalities are important, or something.*

"It just...um...really means a lot, and..."

She stumbled over her words as the fan's breeze tousled her hair. I could only imagine how hard she was fighting to express herself to me. "Yeah?" I asked, prompting her to continue.

Trembling, she hung her head like a sad puppy. If I had to guess, no amount of careful planning would help her speak coherently. She lacked experience in every category, and it was possibly too late to bridge that gap. But the words that *did* make it through her rigorous screening process always touched my heart. Perfection was by no means required.

"I...I'll do my best!"

In the end, she skipped over all the careful agonizing and finished with a declaration that was just...so very Adachi. It really put a smile on my face. Somehow I knew more or less exactly what she was trying to say. This was an important relationship for the both of us.

So I knelt down, pressed my palms to the floor, and bowed humbly.

"I'm looking forward to this too."

It felt weird to say, but also oddly fulfilling. Maybe it would be fun to let myself buy into the illusion of it all.

Before long, it came time to head to school.

"Are you gonna skip school again?" asked my sister.

"I shall await my souvenir in the form of donuts!" exclaimed Yashiro.

"No to both of you," I replied.

Adachi had already bolted out of the house; I stepped outside and found her waiting dutifully with her bike, which she promptly dragged over. Sideways.

"Can I put my bag in the basket?"

"Oh, sure." She hastily removed her own. *We can both share, you know,* I thought with a wry smirk as I placed both of our bookbags into the basket.

With nothing to carry, I started walking. Two steps later, however, I realized Adachi hadn't started pedaling. Confused, I looked back at her.

She wiggled her rear tire. "Do you wanna...?"

"Ride on the back?"

"Uh, yeah... I-I'm gonna pedal real hard! Ha ha..." She was trying to make a joke, but her timing was off, and it didn't land. Still, I didn't really mind.

And so I dropped all pretense of being an honor student and hopped on the back of her bike. With my feet on her rear axle and my hands on her shoulders, it felt like I'd gone back in time...except her shoulders weren't as stiff back then.

"You sure you're not out of shape after that long vacation?"

"Well, uh... No, it's okay! You're not that heavy! Heh... heh heh..."

I could tell she was trying to be considerate, and I would have given her full marks if only she hadn't stumbled at the start.

"Hee hee hee..."

"Heh heh heh..."

And so off we went, wind and sunshine in our faces. Today marked the start of the second semester, and the two of us were starting it together. The bike soared down the street, carrying twice its usual load. As long as we maintained our balance, it'd be smooth sailing all the way to the school building.

I could get used to this. Maybe she could pick me up every day... Then again, I couldn't make Adachi be my chauffeur all the time. After all, she was my girlfriend. It just wasn't right, you know?

"Hmmmm..."

So far, nothing between us felt very different at all. Surely *something* was supposed to change now that we were dating, right? As Adachi steered the bike, I zoned out and gave it some thought. It was a complicated

question, to be sure, and it wasn't easy to always be perfectly mindful of these things. Truth be told, very few of my relationships were ever more than superficial...so how was I meant to treat my girlfriend?

I mulled it over all the way to school. As a result, I forgot to hop off before we passed through the front gates, but luckily, we made it to the bike parking area without getting scolded by any teachers. Then we slowed to a stop, and I stepped off. But right as I straightened up, an idea occurred to me.

"Shimamura?"

I peeled Adachi's slender fingers off the handlebar and gazed down at them. "Sakura," I called experimentally.

Her eyes widened, and she froze. Then she recoiled so sharply, you'd think somebody hit her. Her shoulders shook, and I could hear her sputtering as she hid her face in her arms—was she coughing? Suppressing the desire to tickle her unguarded armpits, I waited for her to recover.

Good thing no other students came to park their bikes. An outside observer would totally think I punched her in the face.

"Uh...you okay, sweetie?"

She was coughing like her favorite mineral water had

gone down the wrong pipe, and I was starting to feel bad. Maybe I shouldn't have sprung it on her out of nowhere... but then again, if I asked in advance, it wouldn't have any emotional impact. What was more important: romance or my girlfriend's well-being?

Hm. This is complicated.

Meanwhile, she finally recovered. Tears had sprung to her eyes—from the pain, I had to assume—and those damp doe eyes made me flustered in return.

"I'm really sorry."

"No, no, it's fine," she sniffled. *Girl, if you're dripping snot everywhere, then this is clearly not fine.*

She reached out and timidly ran her finger over my palm, almost like she was practicing the alphabet. It was very tickly. Then she looked up at me and said...

"H-Hougetsu."

"That's me," I answered with a bright smile. She hunched her shoulders and blushed. Like a shy little Adachi turtle.

"Doesn't really roll off the tongue."

"Tell me about it."

Nobody named their kid Hougetsu these days. I couldn't imagine what life would be like if she started calling me that all the time.

"Sorry, Shimamura, but I really think Shimamura fits the best."

"Yeah, maybe so." It was certainly what I was used to being called. And likewise—to me, she was just *Adachi*.

Obviously, we couldn't stand around here forever, so I started walking, but our hands were still linked. Confused, I looked at her—but she blinked back at me too. Maybe she didn't consciously realize she'd laced her fingers with mine.

For some reason, she always got so fidgety whenever I looked at her... Was I really that intimidating? *No, that's not it.* Knowing her, it was probably the *whole concept of dating* that was intimidating.

"H-Hou-chan?" Adachi croaked stiffly, trying out a new nickname.

"Wow. No one's ever called me that."

"Then what about, like...Shima-chan, or something?"

"Urk...!"

At the very least, it was clear she was trying to be considerate of my comfort level, and I quietly applauded her efforts.

We had arrived at school early, so no one else was wandering the halls. As a result, we ended up holding hands all the way to the classroom door. But as one might expect, we couldn't exactly waltz into the classroom hand in hand, so this was where I pulled away.

Of course, instead of kowtowing to cultural norms, I *did* have the option of taking a defiant stance in direct opposition to society. But I wasn't sure we could survive with the whole world against us. Well, actually, we probably could, but... *Hmm. It just doesn't feel right. Eh, whatever.*

Adachi smiled back at me longingly, then made a request in exchange: "Could you say it one more time?"

"Say what?"

"My name..."

She stared down at the floor, forgetting to even blink. Without even touching her, I could tell that her heart was pounding. Truth be told, I was a tiny bit jealous. I wished it felt real for me too, but it didn't yet.

"Sakura," I called, just as requested.

As if on cue, her cheeks flushed an apt shade of cherry-blossom pink. But she seemed to be adapting to it, because this time, she didn't sputter.

After everything that had happened this morning,

plus the mild sleep deprivation, I found myself nodding off during the entrance ceremony.

"Blegh..."

The next thing I knew, the day was over. I packed my bookbag and contemplated going home to take a nap. Come to think of it, Gon was always taking naps too... *Maybe I'm a little old grandma already,* I thought to myself with a chuckle.

Speaking of grandmothers, mine sent me emails every now and then, usually with photos of Gon attached. Sometimes they were normal and sometimes they were weird; nevertheless, every time I opened one, I felt emotions spiral in my heart. Not all of them were positive, but I could tell they were strong. This change scared me—a chill ran down my spine, and I could feel an incomprehensible sensation in my gut, like mild nausea.

"Blegh."

Time to go home.

Just then, I noticed a shadow hovering over my desk. I looked up and found Adachi standing beside me. She tugged gently on my shirt sleeve, reminiscent of the way my little sister acted whenever we were in public. "Can... can we leave school together?"

"Sure, I don't mind." *Though it'll only last until we reach the front gates.*

"Wh-what I mean is...I'll take you home."

"Oh...?"

"Well, because you're m-my gir—"

"Right! Okay, then! Let's go!" Planting my hands on her shoulders, I steered her out into the hall before she could make an accidental proclamation right there in the middle of the classroom. *I swear, she's such a handful.*

"Whoa, whoa, whoa!" Adachi looked a little flustered, but seemed to be enjoying our spontaneous two-person conga line. She was smiling, albeit stiffly.

Jeez, why is she so bad at smiling? I guess she hasn't had much practice... Maybe I should try to make her smile...? I eyed the loose-fitting sleeves of her summer uniform and briefly contemplated tickling her armpits, but decided that wouldn't count. *Gosh, her arms sure are pale. It's like she skipped summer altogether.*

Outside the school building, I could see a petite girl and a curvy girl walking just up ahead. They heard us walk out and turned to look.

"Hey there, Shima-chee and Ada-chee!"

"Chee!"

Would it kill you to try a little harder, Nagafuji?

78

"Chee," I replied, testing it out. Oddly enough, it was actually kind of perfect—just the right amount of friend-liness without too much effort. It was a fun little in-joke.

Nagafuji hadn't changed since the last time I saw her, but Hino was tanned to a crisp, just like my sister. Apparently, the sunshine in Hawaii was just as effective as ours.

"I see you don't have much of a tan. What'd you do over summer break?"

"Eh, the usual. Homework."

"Hah! Good one."

Wow, Hino doesn't even believe me.

If I looked them in the eye and told them I got my-self a girlfriend, Hino would surely flip out. Nagafuji, though? She'd probably start clapping. Honestly, was there *anything* that could throw her for a loop? She was always as cool as a cucumber.

"Oh, that reminds me, Shimamura-cheechee."

"Hold the 'chees,' Hino. What's up?"

"Your mom came by Nagafuji's store yesterday."

"Yeah, I know." *Because she served their croquettes at din-ner.* "But how do *you* know that?" *Not like it's your house.*

At this, Nagafuji chuckled smugly and adjusted her glasses. "Did you get potatoes stuck in your teeth?"

79

"...What exactly are you hoping I'll say to that...?"

Weirdo. I smiled in spite of myself. Then I noticed Adachi hadn't said anything, so I looked over, and our eyes met. Unsurprisingly—*unsurprisingly?!*—she wasn't smiling even a little. I tried waving my hand in front of her face. She grabbed me by the wrist and started dragging me off.

"Whoa, whoa, whoa!"

Hino and Nagafuji stared after us in surprise but were otherwise understanding. "See you around!"

"Smell you later!"

Ah, a vintage pop culture reference. I waved goodbye, and we parted ways.

Adachi dragged me all the way to the bike parking area without looking back. When I timidly peered at her to find out if she was upset, I saw that her gaze was darting around awkwardly. She seemed to recognize that she was acting out of line but had committed herself to doing it anyway; I looked around at the bikes, then up at the sky. *I think I might know what's going on here.*

"Uhhh... Are you jealous?" *Because I was talking to other girls?*

She shook her head vigorously.

"Ada-chee?"

"No I'm not-chee!"

The look on your face says you are-chee. I chuckled in mild exasperation, but then she whirled around to face me, her hands clenched into fists. *Whoa.* I recoiled slightly.

"I'm not jealous...but..." A streak of pink ran across her cheeks as she pouted her lips like a sulking child. "You're not allowed to...to cheat on me."

"What? *That*? That counts as cheating?"

She nodded slightly. "Because you're...m-my girl-friend..."

"That's true." And Adachi was *my* girlfriend. *So complicated.* "Okay, well, I think your expectations might be a little too strict..."

"No, they're not!" She shouted so firmly, she made the peeling paint on the bike rack flutter. I felt my smile harden. Then Adachi realized she had bared her fangs at me and slowly shrank into herself once more. "I...I respectfully disagree."

Now she was back to being her usual "fearful squirrel" self. Again, her shoulders were so hunched, you'd think I punched her in the face. But there was no undoing what had happened, and I could feel people starting to stare. That, however, was something I was willing to set aside for now.

"Okay, then..." I trailed off awkwardly. Then I reached out and squished her cheeks.

"Whpphh?!"

She looked at me in alarm, but I kept on squishing. Her skin was nice and cool at first, but over time, it started to heat up. Next, I stretched her cheeks out as far as they would go.

"Hhhmmrra?!"

If I had to guess, she was probably calling my name. Maybe.

"Hmmmm..."

I pretended to think long and hard while I squished and squeezed. This was my way of wrecking the tension. And since I was making an effort to cheer her up, maybe I was acting like a proper boyfriend... *Wait, why should I have to be a "boyfriend" at all?*

This did nothing to solve the actual problem, but it achieved my short-term goal. It was the best I could do for today. Hopefully, Future Me could take it from here.

And so the second semester officially began. This marked the end of 24/7 bedtime (in other words, my escape from the daily alarm clock), and the fireworks had fizzled out. From now on, every Monday, I would embark on a long journey to the upcoming weekend.

That holy Saturday afternoon, I was eating a sandwich and watching TV when they aired an interview about a girl my age. I was only half-paying attention, so I missed some of the details, but apparently she performed extra well in her extracurricular activity. She eagerly explained to the camera that she viewed her time in high school as an opportunity to better herself, and she was excited to see her hard work paying off.

"I guess not all teenagers are as lazy as you," my mother snarked as she walked by carrying the laundry.

Yes, Mother, I'm aware that I'm lazy. Hmph.

"But das okie, 'cuz I wuv my wazy wittle Hougetsu-chan!"

"Mom, you're digging your chin into my scalp. It hurts."

And so, stealing a quick bite of my sandwich, she walked off. Apparently, that was her primary target right from the start. I took another bite and went back to watching TV, but the interview had already ended.

"An opportunity to better myself, huh...?"

It certainly sounded empowering...but I was already at my limits just dragging my beaten carcass from one day to the next. How had I spent my time thus far, and what would I invest it in going forward? It was Adachi who held the answer to that, not me.

"My dear, jealous girlfriend... Ha ha ha..."

It wasn't really anything to laugh about. Especially if things got any worse. *Ha ha.*

Adachi loved me and all, but what she wanted wasn't touchy-feely kissy stuff. I got the sense that she just wanted to feel special. Probably because no one else in her life ever treated her that way. That much I understood... and yet...if she kept trying to tie me down so tightly, I was going to turn into a boneless ham. And she was going to gobble me up.

"Eeek... Scary..." *Nom, nom.*

"Oh, hello, Shimamura-san!"

Then Yashiro came toddling into the room. This carefree kid didn't have a single thing holding her down—no worries, no gravity, and no ulterior motives. Lately, I was starting to envy her.

"Ooh! I see you're eating something marvelous." Her eyes went straight to my food. "And that was the day I learned about egg salad sandwiches..."

For some reason she was narrating aloud, all the while waiting beside me with a hopeful grin. But what I found funny—or rather, interesting—was the fact that if I chose not to share my sandwich, she wouldn't get mad at me. The last time I turned her down for whatever reason, all she said to me was "What a crying shame indeed!" and then she skipped off somewhere. She didn't hold it against me later either.

Maybe this was to be expected, considering she was just a mooch at our house, but to me, it was an impressive feat to take disappointment on the nose and shrug it off without complaint. Kids vented their anger outwardly, adults learned healthy coping mechanisms, and those of us caught in the middle simply bottled it up. But Yashiro didn't fit in any of those boxes. She remained unaffected, like a glacier from the Ice Age.

"Here." I offered her the rest of my sandwich.

"Woohoo!" She gleefully pounced and started chomping. Would Adachi count this as cheating too? I was basically just feeding a stray... *Oh, so that's why we can never get rid of her.* I had made a careless mistake, and now it was too late.

"You really savor your food, don't you?"

"Af crrsh ah ddh."

"Settle down, now. Don't bite my fingers off."

She seemed too perfect to be real, both inside and out. Where on earth did this innocent little creature come from?

"Say, have you ever felt jealous?"

"Personally, I prefer jam to jelly."

"Ha ha ha..." *Of course.*

In the end, she ate every last bite of my sandwich.

"Hmmm... Guess I'll give it a try."

"Huh?"

As she savored the aftertaste, I left her behind and went to fetch my phone. In the bedroom, I found my sister diligently working on her homework.

"You're being so responsible! I'm proud of you."

"Yeah, well, not all of us are like *you*, Nee-chan."

"Oh, really?"

"Gyaaah!"

After I tormented my bratty sister's plump cheeks, I dialed Ada-chee's number. It barely rang once before she answered, which was impressive. *If she was a contestant on a game show, she'd probably be real good at buzzing in.*

"Hello?!"

"You don't have to run to the phone," I scolded her. I could tell from her breathy voice that she had probably leapt all the way across the room. She was just so *obvious.*

"Well, it's just... It's not every day that *you* call *me*, so..."

Frankly, her ability to adapt to unexpected situations was nothing to sneeze at. "Is it really that uncommon?"

"Uh, yeah?" Her voice sounded ever so faintly pouty, and I quickly realized this was not a subject I should attempt to broach.

"Well, you see, Adachi-san..."

"Yeah?!"

I could hear the anticipation in her tone, like she was hoping I might ask her to hang out. I wasn't opposed to it, of course, but that was hardly anything new for us, and I felt it was time we started taking baby steps into uncharted territory.

"Would you wanna make lunch for each other?"

"Huh?"

"I was thinking I could pack a lunch for you, and you could pack a lunch for me."

See? Girlfriend stuff, am I right? Honestly, I considered just surprising her with it, but Adachi didn't handle surprises too well. If she started sputtering in the classroom, we'd attract unwanted attention. Besides, it wouldn't be fair if I was the only one who had to make something. *We're both girlfriends, after all.*

"You're...going to cook for me...?" she asked in a watery voice. "That sounds great... Yeah, really great."

She seemed to like this suggestion even more than I expected. I was thinking it was maybe a bit too simplistic, but apparently not.

"So...you're going to make something for me?" she pressed.

"I will. But don't forget, *you* have to make something too, missy!"

"Yeah...yeah..." With a response like that, it was hard to say whether she was actually listening. "But...can you even cook, Shimamura?"

"Ha ha ha!" *Sure, I can play it your way.* "Can *you*?"

Granted, I knew she worked at a Chinese restaurant, but as far as I knew, she was just a waitress.

"Well, uh...I've made chocolate before..."

"Whoa." Personally, I couldn't say the same, and it sounded pretty impressive. Come to think of it, didn't she send me pictures of chocolates last February? Was that what she was talking about?

"I...I'm sure it'll be fine. For both of us. Even if your food doesn't turn out perfect, I'll still eat it, Shimamura."

"Very reassuring, thank you."

Frankly, I wasn't planning to try too hard, so I wasn't worried about anything catastrophic happening. Having successfully made plans with her, I ended the call.

"Now then..." I walked down the hall, thinking of things I could feasibly make, and peeked into the living room. "Ah, there we go."

"I beg your pardon?"

I took one look at Yashiro lounging on the floor and immediately thought of sandwiches. *Perfect*. Rather than flying too close to the sun and getting burned, I was better off sticking to something simple that I could reasonably manage. If I had to guess, what mattered most to Adachi was that I made something for her by hand.

"Are you available, Shimamura-san?" Yashiro slithered over to my feet like a snake, her eyes sparkling hopefully up at me from the floor.

"Go play with my sister."

"Little is busy with her homework."

"Oh, that's right... Okay, then, why not read some manga?"

I was free earlier, but now I was busy. Busy with Adachi. And for better or for worse, this was only going to happen more often from now on.

"You make a good point. It couldn't hurt to brush up on my language skills," she nodded. *That wasn't why I suggested it, but okay.*

We had so much manga in this house, everything that couldn't fit on the bookshelf was packed into a cardboard box. When I handed her a few volumes, she raised them over her head and ran off to find my sister in our bedroom. Such good friends, those two.

Was it Yashiro's carefree personality that helped my shy sister open up? Part of me wanted to take a page out of her book, but at the same time, it felt like too little, too late. I wasn't a kid anymore; I had already grown into a defective teenager. And with every passing year, it became harder and harder to follow my heart when there were so many rules, obligations, and expectations to follow instead.

"It's important to review your textbooks, after all..."

Growing up, we were supposed to learn the importance of *understanding others* and *doing for others*. And right now, I wanted to test it out for myself.

The purpose of having days off was to give the body a chance to rest. People achieved this in a variety of ways; some rested physically, while others ran around freely and gave their minds a rest instead. So while other people saw me as a sleepy little sloth, in actuality, I was just a strong proponent of "self-care" or whatever. So I ignored the rising sun and sank deeply back to sleep. I wanted to lose myself to the passage of time.

"Geddup!"

"Guh!"

Just like that, the blanket was ripped—or peeled?—away, yanking me out of sleep's embrace. I could understand if it was a weekday, but *why*, pray tell, couldn't I sleep in on a weekend? I blinked at my mother in drowsy confusion. She jerked her thumb over her shoulder at the open door.

"Ugh..." I craned my neck to look out at the hallway. Nothing was there except bright sunshine.

"You've got a visitor."

"A visitor...?"

I left the darkness afforded by my blackout curtains and staggered out into the hall, still in my PJs. The sunshine streamed into my eyes until I couldn't see a thing. As I approached the front door, however, my mind sharpened enough to realize who this "visitor" probably was.

Sure enough, when I opened the door, Adachi was standing there, carrying a huge bag of stuff. On a Sunday.

"...Whoa, whoa, whoa. Hold on a minute."

This was a sneak attack, and I was *not* prepared. I could guess why she was here, but...why was her bag so big?

"When I said 'make lunches for each other,' I meant, like...at school...on Monday or something." Did she think I meant we were going on a picnic? *Hmmm.*

92

Incidentally, her shirt read LOVE BITES.

Indeed it does. And so does your sense of timing.

"I haven't even made anything for you yet."

"Oh, no, no! This is, uh, practice!"

"Practice?"

"And research. I wanna find out what you think about this stuff."

The straps digging into her shoulders told me everything I needed to know. "Classic Adachi…" Cautious, yet proactive.

The lid of her thermos glinted dully in the sun as it peeked out from inside the overstuffed bag. What on earth had she made for me? I had already eaten breakfast, but I was still curious.

"Well, at least this way we'll be able to eat in peace, I guess." She would probably feel more comfortable in private, anyway. I bit back a yawn. "Come on in."

Dating Adachi naturally meant more social activity. This applied to weekends as well as weekdays, steadily eroding my sleep time…and as someone who only felt at peace when I was asleep, I didn't entirely approve. But as I gazed into Adachi's giddy eyes, I found myself swayed. *Eh, why not?*

"Welcome," my mother greeted as she swept the hallway.

She glanced at Adachi's giant bag and cocked her head. "Are you here for another bath?"

"Wha...?! No, I..."

"She packed a lunch and invited me to eat some."

"*Here*? Why?"

Adachi turned pink.

Then my mother looked at me. "Interesting friendship you've got here."

"Yeah, I guess." That was certainly the most optimistic way of interpreting Adachi's unpredictable behavior.

"*Packed a lunch*... Now that takes me back! I haven't packed a lunch for you in like a year or something, huh?" My mother laughed cheerfully. *Is that something you should be proud of, Mom?*

"You could always start up again," I suggested. Not like I asked her to stop.

"Noooo!" she pouted childishly. I ignored her and headed up the stairs.

"You really take after your mom, huh, Shimamura?" Adachi commented as she followed suit.

"I do?" I ran a hand over my cheekbones and nose. *I guess so.* "Well, at least I'm not as weird as her on the inside."

"You sure?"

"What? What was that?"

"Nothing!" For once, her tone was firm.

And so I invited her into the study room. We ventilated this room all the time, so how did it always get so dusty overnight? Where did it all come from? I vaguely remembered learning about it in school, but then they said it wouldn't be on the test, so I promptly forgot. Bad habit of mine.

We sat down at the *kotatsu* table, still draped in a heavy winter blanket in the middle of summer. Then Adachi lowered her big bag to the floor. *How much food is even in there?* I wondered, mildly concerned.

"Here." Nervously, she pushed something in my direction.

"Okay..."

I took it. Admittedly, a single dish in a Tupperware container didn't really feel like a "packed lunch" to me. *Wait, but if this is the only food she made, then what else is in the bag...? Meh, whatever.* I popped the lid. Inside was something flat and golden brown.

"Is this...an *okonomiyaki* pancake?" With my chopsticks, I pulled out a piece of green onion that was peeking out.

"I've made them at work before."

"You made Japanese food...at the Chinese restaurant?"

"Yeah."

NANI?!

I used my sticks to chop it up. *Get it? Because they're chopsti—never mind.* Then I lifted it up—and found another pancake underneath. *Well, okay. I can probably eat two.*

"Did you want more than that?" She pulled her bag over, and I had a bad feeling I knew what was coming.

"No, no, I don't think I could eat more than two!"

"Oh." She pushed her bag away again. *Good grief, how much is in there?* Then she pulled out her thermos and poured us some tea.

With everything set up on the table, it reminded me of the days I used to play house as a kid. I would always get bored after five minutes and run off...so I guess I didn't really "play house" at all.

"Here."

"Okay."

This was identical to our earlier exchange. I found myself rolling my sleeves up, even though they weren't that long to begin with. It was my first time eating a classmate's home cooking, and the thrill of the unknown made my heart race. I pressed my hands together to say grace. Then I reached out, plucked a piece with my chopsticks, and brought it to my mouth. *Nom, nom.*

Since Adachi was watching my every move, I wasn't confident I'd be able to swallow, but managed it nonetheless. Then I met her fearful gaze. It felt like her anxiety was contagious.

"Do you want me to be honest, or should I just be nice?" Inadvertently, it sounded like I was calling the food gross.

"How about...s-somewhere in the middle...?"

Somewhere in the middle, hmm? "Well...it's cold."

"Oh, uh...!" Hastily, she grabbed her bag and pulled out a ton of identical Tupperware containers. *Ugh, I knew it! I totally knew it!* She felt all the containers in turn, then chose one. "Um, I think these ones are a little warmer."

I opened its lid for a taste-test. "Yeah, this one's good."

Fried food just didn't taste the same after it went cold, but this one was much better. *Dang, she can really cook*, I thought to myself, mildly impressed. My only critique was the, uh, *portion size.* Just when I was starting to wonder who was going to have to eat all the rest, she sidled over to me.

"Adachi?"

"Ahhh..."

She moaned sensually—*just kidding*. She opened her mouth. I had a feeling I knew what she was asking for, so I grabbed a piece of *okonomiyaki* in my chopsticks...but before I fed her, I peeked into her open mouth. It was a rare sight, after all. *Ooh, her gums are bright pink.* Or maybe it was just the contrast with her pearly white teeth.

"Um...can you hurry up...?"

"You've got green onion in your teeth."

She clacked her teeth together, urging me to get on with it. I didn't want her to bite me if I messed around too much, so I acquiesced. But where to put it? Onto her tongue? As I gingerly slid it into her mouth, her tongue curled around the bite of food. *Mission successful!* I pulled my chopsticks away.

"How is it?" *Wait, but I didn't cook this!*

"Good."

For some reason, she looked really satisfied. Though her gaze was averted, she couldn't fully conceal her smile. Sure, it was an odd lunch, but if it made us both happy, then what was the harm?

"Now it's my turn."

As she spoke, she reached out to take my chopsticks— but just then, my phone started to ring from the corner of the table where I left it. But if Adachi was here, then who could be calling...?

Oh, right. Tarumi. I forgot.

"Whoops! I'm getting a call!" Casually, I grabbed my phone. Sure enough, it was Tarumi. "Just a sec, okay?"

But Adachi didn't respond—she just stared at me intently. *Good grief.* I left the room and answered the call.

"Hello?"

"Oh, hey there, Shima-chan!" I hadn't heard Tarumi's voice in ages—since I declined her festival invitation. "Uhhh, so...good morning."

"Good morning!" I answered as I walked down the stairs.

"I'll cut to the chase. Are you free right now?"

"Wellllll..." Then I heard a soft sound over my shoulder. "One sec, okay?"

"Huh?"

I headed back up the stairs and hissed, "*Hey!*"

There was a startled rustle, as if I'd tossed a rock into a still lake. After a moment, the door opened, and Adachi slowly revealed herself. Like a child caught misbehaving, she looked up at me with puppy-dog eyes. "But..."

"No buts, missy!" I lightly karate-chopped her on the head. The shadow of my hand fell across her side part. "Look, you don't have to be all sneaky, you know."

"Huh? You mean like...I should eavesdrop right next to you?"

"No, that's not what I mean!" *How do I explain it...? Maybe it'd be better to express it through actions... I get the general gist of what she wants, so... Okay, let's do it.*

I combed her bangs up and planted a kiss on her forehead. I could feel a slight depression against my lips. *Sheesh, she's so skinny.*

When I pulled away, she remained frozen in place, kneeling and recoiling. As for her face... Well, it wasn't much different from the usual. Bright red like a strawberry.

"You're the only person I do these things with." At the moment, anyway. When was the last time I kissed anybody's forehead? I used to kiss my sister back when she was in diapers, and since she and Adachi were similar, I figured it would be effective.

In actuality, however, it was perhaps a little *too* effective.

"Believe me now?"

At my question, she shrank back and nodded, twice.

Good. I shooed her back into the study room. "This won't take long."

She nodded in understanding, then retreated back into the room like an injured bird scrambling to safety. It reminded me of that night at the festival.

"Shima-chan?"

I resumed the phone call. "Sorry. I've got a friend over at my house right now."

"Oh...I see. Then I guess I should...call back later?"

"Uhhh...yeah, I guess so. Yeah. Sorry." The apology felt dry and tasteless on my tongue.

"Okay, talk to you later..."

"Bye..."

One step forward, two steps back. As a faint hint of awkwardness returned to the air, I ended the call and quietly despised myself for, even briefly, thinking of a girl who was supposed to be my friend as *annoying*.

"Nope. I need to stop that." I scratched my head, scolding myself. "Ugh, I hate this." I hated feeling like I was an unfeeling monster. "But...I guess I am."

With my muted emotions, perhaps "unfeeling" was the most apt way to describe me. With limited emotional range, my ability to care was shallow at most—pleasant and light-hearted at a surface level, but with absolutely no depth. That was why, every now and then when I *did* find myself full of emotion, it ripped a hole in me. My heart was as flimsy as a goldfish scoop.

In my grandma's eyes, I was witty, beautiful, and fair-minded...or something like that. But when it came to

Adachi, being impartial probably wasn't the right move. She was my girlfriend, after all; I was allowed—no, *expected*—to be a little biased in her favor. But if I let myself do that, then my scant few emotions would all lean to one side. Someone would inevitably get hurt. Even if that imbalance made me uncomfortable, my only option was to overcome it.

Honestly, I wasn't sure this new mindset was going to stick. I'd have to make a conscious effort.

The flow of power was dictated by position, and the relationship between two positions would inevitably create feelings. Take my mother, for example: if she wasn't my mother, then I'd only think of her as an obnoxious adult woman. Therefore, now that Adachi was my girlfriend, something about my behavior needed to change. I just needed to figure out what that "something" was.

I went back into the study room, where Adachi sat cross-legged on the floor, gingerly rubbing her forehead. When she saw me walk in, she hastily lowered her hand. *What, did I get some spit on you? I don't have cooties, you know.*

When I sat down, for some reason, she got up. I looked up at her in confusion. Then she inserted herself in the gap between me and the table. Unfortunately, this was not refreshing in the least. A mass of heat had now propped itself up against me. Experimentally, I touched a finger to her bicep. Yep, she was practically on fire.

"You're such a needy little baby," I sighed.

"Is that a problem?" she asked in a pouty voice.

She only ever acted like this on rare occasions. I didn't mind it in theory, but in a closed-off space, it was sweltering... Of course, knowing her, she probably preferred it this way. Here between my legs, she had found a place to belong.

Using my chopsticks, I took a few more bites of *okonomiyaki*, pausing now and then to give some to Adachi. It wasn't easy to eat in this position, but I found myself thinking it made for an interesting change of pace. It reminded me of the time I used to spend with Gon in my lap.

Oh, Adachi, you're such a little puppy dog. Her eyes and mouth quivered, and the hand she had placed on my leg started to shake.

"Sh-Shimamura...I love you...!" she squeaked out shakily. Her struggle was heartwarming.

"Why, thank you."

She was the first person outside of my own family to feel so strongly about me, and quite possibly, she would be the last. Someday, I would feel grateful that it was her.

Not today, but...someday.

I could only pray that I would soon learn to cherish every second with her...and that I wouldn't need more than a moment's respite in between.

interlude

Hino and Nagafuji

"**O**H, I WAS actually right!"

I looked up from my idle fishing line and saw Nagafuji standing there. For a moment, her head blocked out the sun, but as she approached, it got bright again. The frames of her glasses glinted in the sunlight streaming over her shoulders, and her T-shirt bore the word DISCIPLE in glossy print. *Not mine, I hope.*

"Heyo. What brings you all the way out here?" I asked, raising a hand in greeting.

This was an uncommon sight. Usually, she refused to fish with me, since it was "too boring." One time, I forced her to tag along with me anyway, but I quickly learned my lesson. I couldn't get any fishing done with her around.

"I went to your house, but they told me you had gone fishing."

Her words left a silent implication: *So I chased you all the way here.* Only Nagafuji would come to a fishing hole empty-handed.

"You went to my house? You could have told me you were coming over." *Cell phones are a thing that exist, you know.*

"If I'd told you I was coming, you would've shown up at my house instead."

"You know me well."

Instead of inviting her over to my place, I preferred going to hers. At *her* house, I could actually relax. Not that I hated my family or anything—I just wasn't naturally inclined to live in a huge, empty house. Every now and then I wished someone would come along, reel me in, and put me in their bucket... Then again, actual fish probably didn't enjoy the experience very much, did they?

Nagafuji crouched down beside me and stared out blankly at the still waters. The sunlight still carried the earthy smell of summer, and for a weekend, there weren't many lines cast. That was why I was hoping to relax out here, but alas... I shot her a quick glance.

The reason I couldn't fish with her around was because

she always made things difficult for me. She would stay quiet for about five minutes, then start pinching my cheeks or resting her chin on my head or slapping my legs. She just couldn't be trusted to sit still.

"Today, I'm going to take part in your favorite hobby, just for you."

"Condescending much?"

"In exchange, *you* have to try *my* favorite hobby too."

"Uhh...sure, whatever," I replied offhandedly. Then it hit me. "What *is* your favorite hobby, anyway?"

We always spent so much time doing random stuff together, I'd never really stopped to consider it until now, and I was drawing a blank.

"Who, me? Heh heh." She thrust her chest out smugly for...some reason. "Clearly, you need to do a little more research if you can't answer such basic trivia about me."

"Cram it."

"My favorite hobby is *boomerang throwing*, of course!"

"Oh, that's right. I remember now."

"And my second favorite hobby is caring for you," she declared proudly. But frankly, this was no secret to me.

"...You mean that same stuff you always make me do with you?"

"That's right."

Well, then, I already do it with you all the time! What more do you want from me, you weirdo?

The water rippled quietly as I reeled in my line and packed up my stuff.

"I quit. Let's go home," I announced as I rose to my feet. She looked up at me, partway through a yawn, mouth hanging open.

"What the? Already?"

"Well, you're bored, right?"

"Yeah."

Thus, there was no point in us staying here.

"Oh, and when I said 'go home,' I meant *your* home."

"Noooo! How come?!"

Because lunch at my house was always light, and I wanted to eat something with actual *flavor* for a change. Why did my brothers all eat that rabbit food anyway? Because it was "traditional"? Yeah, probably. Sometimes it was important to carry out the role given to you, and you couldn't always turn a blind eye to it. These things all meshed together to create a functional society.

After we left the fishing hole, Nagafuji took her glasses off and put them away.

"You sure that's safe? I know you're not totally blind without 'em, but..."

To me, *this* was the real Nagafuji. Probably because I first met her before she got glasses, back in elementary school. That said, we were closer to the same height back then.

"I remembered why it is that I wear these glasses."

"Huh? Because you have bad eyesight, right?"

"Yes, yes."

"You really confuse me sometimes..."

"It's because you're so small, Hino."

"Say that again? And wipe that smirk off your face!" I glared back at her.

"I wear my glasses so I can find you in the distance."

I froze, still glaring. She turned and faced forward, her expression peaceful. Her gaze was pointed in the direction of the old, grimy elementary school building.

"So when you're nearby, I don't need them anymore."

"...Good grief. Quit joking around."

Such a weirdo. I started scratching my head, but then she grabbed my hand and pulled me toward her.

"Wh-where did *that* come from?"

"I reeled you in! Yaaaay!"

She whipped our joined hands over her head, yanking me upward onto my tiptoes. Did she get even taller? For a moment, I panicked. *Why does she keep growing?*

*Maybe my family needs to serve more meat at dinnertime...
But then again, my parents and brothers are all taller
than me...*

And so the two of us ended up holding hands as we
walked.

"Can't really remember the last time we held hands."

"Me either."

It felt like we'd done a bunch of this stuff completely
out of order.

"It's nice!"

"Except it's making me sweaty."

From the cicadas to the shape of the clouds, every tiny
detail of summer was slowly being peeled away—*except*
the eternally robust heat. Now that the sun's bright rays
had warmed our town like a microwave, it would take a
little time to cool down again. In the meantime, her palm
was just too hot.

"That's what I like about it," she replied with a smile.

For a moment I wondered: *Why?* But after a few
moments of walking in silence with our joined hands
swinging in the breeze...

"...I guess it's not so bad."

And so I decided to try out one of Nagafuji's favorite
hobbies...at least until we made it back to her house.

In the window's reflection, I was smiling. In the bath-water's reflection, I was grinning. And in the mirror's reflection, I was very clearly smirking.

I was undeniably on cloud nine.

3. Imperfect Words

HONESTLY, WAS I WRONG to want Shimamura to focus only on me? Lately, I was starting to question myself a tiny little bit. Her stiff smile had created ripples in my heart. I wanted that smile to be sweet and pure! I mean, it was always *sweet*, but sometimes it would turn... you know...*hard*.

But what could be more important than focusing on the one thing that mattered most? And I *did* matter most. I was her girlfriend now, after all.

Her girlfriend... Hee hee...

In a blink, our homeroom teacher had finished speaking. My eyes wandered over the words scrawled widely across the blackboard:

"School trip...?"

Apparently, it was happening next month. I had no idea until just now.

Truth be told, I couldn't remember any of the field trips I went on in elementary or junior high school. Couldn't even tell you where we went—all I could recall was the intense desire to go home. But this time was different. This time, I would be with Shimamura...and the thought was enough to crank my excitement up a notch.

Trips are so great... I hope someday Shimamura and I can go on a trip together, just the two of us...

Just then, I made eye contact with the girl in question. She was looking at me through the crowd of students milling about during the break period between classes. Shyly, she raised her hand in a tiny wave. This slight gesture made my chest ache deeply. Taking care to control myself, I waved back.

Since the start of the second semester, Shimamura was all I ever thought about, even during class. Same as before, except more clearly now. It was like holding a flower up to eye level to admire it; the beauty was right in front of me.

Frankly, if I wasn't careful, I was in danger of bursting into song. In fact, my mother had already caught me humming the other day, and she gave me a weird look. Then she asked if I was in a good mood, to which I said,

"No, uh…just average!" Looking back, I felt a little guilty that I hadn't tried to open up and have more of a conversation with her. But my mother rarely ever asked me anything, so I panicked.

Then again, I wouldn't want her to be chatty like Shimamura's mom either…

Shimamura resembled her mother quite a bit, and not just physically—they had some personality traits in common too. I couldn't put my finger on it exactly, but they were both…outwardly cheerful while somewhat detached on the inside…? I couldn't quite express it in words. So I agonized over it all through class without managing to take a single note.

When lunchtime rolled around, I grabbed my bookbag and headed to Shimamura's desk. She greeted me as she was packing up her school supplies.

Since the start of the second semester, the two of us had spent every lunch period together. Incidentally, today we were having *okonomiyaki* pancakes again. There were still six more to go, and Shimamura refused to make lunch until we finished them. "After all, it'd be such a waste to throw them away," she had said. But since she agreed to help me eat them, I couldn't really complain.

After I sat down on the other side of her desk, we

popped the lid on the Tupperware container. I had made sure to reheat the pancakes just this morning, but that was hours ago, and they had gone cold again. Nevertheless, Shimamura ate it up without complaint.

Because you made them for me, Adachi.

...Okay, she didn't actually say that, but...I mean, she probably felt that way, right? Deep down, I was dearly hoping that was the case.

As I joylessly chewed my food, my eyes wandered to Shimamura's lips. Those lips had pressed themselves firmly against my forehead... I couldn't remember all the details since I was too dizzy to see straight, but I knew it definitely happened.

A feverish froth broke out all over my face, enveloping me. That angle, that sensation—it made my heart flutter. But what thrilled me most of all was that she said she'd only do it with *me*. She had absorbed me as a new part of herself, and now our feet were taking turns climbing the stairs... *God, what am I babbling about?* I wasn't sure, but that was the imagery I got.

I hope she does it again, because this time, I'm gonna memorize every last detail, I vowed to myself. Meanwhile, my gaze was fixed on her bewitching lips. Then she noticed me looking at her.

"What's wrong?"

"Nothing! Nothing," I lied hastily, shaking my head and waving my chopsticks.

"Oh, I see how it is," she smirked. *Wait, what?* "Open up and say 'ahhh'!" She plucked up a bite of okonomiyaki and held it out to me with a playful, mischievous grin.

Wh-WHAT?! HERE?!

I glanced around furtively. On one hand, it felt like nobody was looking at us, but on the other hand, it felt like *everybody* was looking at us. In other words, I couldn't see a thing. As the room spun around me, I leaned forward and took the bite. Her chopsticks stabbed into my tongue.

But now that I reflected on the day's events from the safety of my bedroom, I couldn't help but worry that I was letting it all go to my head. I didn't want a repeat of that time I humiliated myself over the phone, so I needed to stay on guard.

"Nope. Can't let that happen."

I slapped my cheeks to wipe the simpering smile off my face. Something similar almost happened at the bike racks, but I managed to stop myself, didn't I? Clearly, I was making progress! Probably! I sat upright on the bed and clenched my hands into fists.

"...But still..."

I wilted and collapsed sideways. While I was fully aware that the blame for the incident was mine alone... who *was* that girl I saw her with at the festival back then? There was nothing Shimamura could say to me that would make me any less curious. I knew I needed to get over it, but after all this time, I still didn't feel at peace.

If I had to guess, it was probably the same girl who called her the other day. Shimamura had a friendship that I wasn't a part of. And I knew this was *perfectly normal* or whatever...but still! I flopped back down onto the bed and rolled back and forth, clutching my face.

Truth be told, I was afraid of the parts of Shimamura I didn't know. I wanted to love every part of her, but to do that, I would need to know everything there was to know about her. To me, that was my life's true purpose. But if I came on too strong, it would make her uncomfortable... It was hard to tell where the line was, and harder still to suppress these impulses I felt.

I rolled violently from side to side like I was on fire, battling my negative emotions. Eventually, once I was sure my desperate yearning had tuckered itself out, I sat back up. All that rolling around had made a mess of my hair.

"I want to see her..."

To make my dreams come true, I would need to put in the effort, one day at a time. Thus, I decided to give her a call and fill at least one of the empty spaces.

"Hello, hello! What's up?"

Shimamura sounded like she was lounging in bed. These days, I could kinda tell, which pleased me, since it felt like proof that I had learned more about her.

"Hey, so, this Sunday..."

"What about it?"

"Let's go on a d-date!" I stammered.

"A d-date, you say?"

"Or it could be just a regular date...with one D..."

"Ha ha ha ha! Wow, you're so flexible!" she joked. Then, a beat later: "Sure. This Sunday, you said? Got it."

"Okay...cool..."

"You could have waited until tomorrow and asked me at school, you know."

A fair point. But I was dying to ask her *now*. "I only just thought of it is all."

"Aha...I see. Well, gosh, I guess that's as good of a reason as any."

"You...you think so?" I always appreciated compliments from Shimamura, even if I didn't always understand where they were coming from.

"So, where do you wanna go?"

"Where...?"

Where can I get you to kiss my forehead? Where do I have to take you? Where?

"Oh, god, you're totally bugging out, aren't you?"

Where?!

"Helloooo? Earth to Adachi!"

WHERE?!

And so a full day had passed.

Resting my elbows on my bedroom desk, I clutched my head in my hands. I could rack my brain all I wanted, but I wasn't going to find something that wasn't there to begin with. I contemplated it all day long until my ears started to ring, but all I achieved was a headache. I debated it over and over until I made myself sick. This was quite possibly the hardest I'd ever thought about something in all my life.

As I lay slumped over the desk, I considered getting some rest but ultimately kept agonizing over it. Did such a place even exist? *Forehead Kiss Café? No such thing. Forehead Kiss Movie Theater? Boring. The Forehead Kiss Store? What would they even sell?* Clearly the "forehead" thing was getting me nowhere. I would just have to rely on Shimamura's natural height advantage—

Wait, no! I'm the one who's taller, not her!

Despite all the head pats and reassurance tricking me into thinking otherwise, I was in fact the taller of us. Was there any date destination where I'd have to crouch down...? *Ugh, what am I even talking about?* What about a place where Shimamura would have to stand on tiptoe? *Now I'm expecting too much.*

Frankly, I was convinced that I was looking at it the wrong way. Instead of looking for a place to cater to my needs, I needed to steer things in that direction with my own two hands. What if I simply asked her to kiss my forehead? My hand gravitated toward my phone.

But then again...wouldn't it be kinda weird? And by "kinda" I mean "extremely"? Or would it be okay? Wouldn't be the first time she thought I was weird... Well, yeah, but I need to work on that...so maybe I shouldn't after all? But if I don't ask her, then I'll have to figure something out during the date...but like what, though?

Questions swirled around and around in my mind, making me dizzy.

For now, let's...let's just call Shimamura.

These days, I had started to crave her voice as soon as I got home from school. Pretty sure all I ever did was look for excuses to call her. I knew she would answer regardless, but what would we talk about? I despised how downright awful I could be at small talk. If only I'd spent more time talking to people over the years—would I be any better at it? Then again, if I was that drastically different, there was no telling whether I would have met Shimamura to begin with.

For better or for worse, my choices had led to this. Me and Shimamura.

She answered the phone after a few rings. "Helloooo?"

"Uh, good evening..."

"Feels like we've been talking on the phone a lot lately."

Startled, I quickly played dumb. "Have we...?"

"Not that I mind. So, what's up today?"

"I wanted to...ask you something..."

"Oh?"

I took a deep breath, then began.

"Whasso...kyuwanna..."

"I can't hear you."

"Wh...sdd...mggyuwah..."

"I really can't decipher that."

I wanted to ask, "What sort of date would make you want to kiss my forehead?" but could only manage to mumble incoherently. (I'll leave the rest to your imagination.) Long story short, she finally grasped what I was getting at.

"*Huh*?" She raised her voice, highlighting her sheer confusion. "What do you mean...? Uhhh, give me a minute."

This was Shimamura at her most perplexed, which wasn't surprising, given the situation. Looking back, I couldn't explain why I said it. But the fact of the matter was, it was keeping me up at night. Clearly, something was wrong with my brain.

In the end, I chose to ask her directly.

"So basically, you want me to kiss your forehead?"

"...Yeah..."

"Silly. All you have to do is ask and I'll... Wait..."

"All I have to do is ask?!" I repeated eagerly.

"Actually, I changed my mind."

"Wha?!"

"Well, you said you're going to convince me during the date, right?" she teased.

Rrrrgh! "Yeah, but I don't think it'll work...which is why I asked..."

"Just do your best!" she replied casually.

Easy for you *to say! Grrrrrr!* I flailed my arms in frustration. That being said, however, I didn't want to beg like a loser. If at all possible, I wanted to earn my reward. And if Shimamura was rooting for me in any capacity, then I wanted to try to meet her expectations.

After the phone call, I checked my call history. Nothing but *Shimamura* all the way down. I counted them all in my head and finally realized just how many phone calls we'd been having lately.

"Hee hee...hee hee hee..."

But I didn't have time to sit around and giggle. I turned to the calendar and started counting. Sunday was six entire days away—my punishment for being too impatient to wait until Friday to ask her. Still, it didn't feel like enough time.

What do I do? What do I do? What would I do normally? What do I do?

"I could...smear whipped cream on my forehead...?"

It was an idiotic idea conceived by the queen of all idiots. In my despair, I buried my face in my hands and listened to the clock ticking.

For better or for worse, time wasn't going to wait for me.

After school, I suppressed the urge to fling myself into Shimamura's arms and speedily left the classroom. When I looked over my shoulder, I caught her staring wide-eyed at me. Then she waved goodbye, so I waved back. I was really tempted to go to her, but I bit it back and headed off to the bookstore.

I sincerely doubted that any modern magazine would have specific advice on how to get a girl to kiss me on the forehead during a date, but I was desperately hoping I might find some sort of hint somewhere. I still had yet to decide where we were going. I couldn't keep taking her to the mall every time or it would lose its novelty...but at the same time, this backwoods town didn't offer a lot of variety.

Internally, I was panicking, but it helped to have an objective in mind. Only now did I become cognizant of the weight in my limbs that would otherwise go unnoticed. I fought it with every motion, urging myself onward. Believe it or not, it was strangely fulfilling. I could feel a strong connection between myself and my bike.

I crossed over the bridge and arrived at the old bookstore, a fairly large brick-red building. After they banned customers from "sampling" the books prior to purchase, I started to notice a few empty spaces in the previously packed parking lot. The big building next door used to sell video games and CDs, but at some point, it had turned into a pharmacy.

I walked in and milled around the first floor. The second floor was where they kept the reference books, manga, and school supplies, so I had no reason to go up there today. I hadn't been here in quite some time; I didn't read many books, and I didn't study enough to warrant new school supplies. Would they have magazines explicitly focused on dating?

Indeed they did, and explicit they were. My face flushed before I could grab anything off the shelf.

Honestly, I wasn't expecting to find what I was looking for this quickly. I grabbed the one that was positioned in the front at eye level: *The Complete Guide to Girlfriends*. Would something like this work? In my case, I wanted to know what sorts of dates girls would like—more specifically, dates *Shimamura* would like. After all, I wanted her to have a fun time, whether I achieved my goal or not.

"Oho..."

Just then, I heard a voice from directly behind me. My mind went blank. Heart pounding in my chest, I whirled around to find yet another surprise waiting for me: a face inches from mine. And judging from the way she was squinting at me, her eyesight was truly terrible.

"Chee-chee, it's you! I knew it!"

She slid her glasses on to confirm. Personally, I would have appreciated it if she'd put them on a lot sooner.

"Uh...hi, Nagafuji..." Was I supposed to call her "Nagafuji-san" to be polite? We weren't especially close, but we weren't total strangers either... I wasn't sure how to gauge the distance between myself and someone who wasn't Shimamura.

But Nagafuji didn't seem to care. She peered down at the magazine in my hands—*oh, crap*. I felt my palms start to sweat. The longer I stood here holding this stupid thing, the more likely it would create some sort of misunderstanding! Not that it *was* a misunderstanding, but... you know what I mean!

"Got a hot *d-date*?"

"Uhhh...don't worry about it. So, uh, where's Hino?"

"Went home early for 'family business.' But *I* do not have any family business!"

Why did she sound so proud of this detail? Also, if she walked all the way here on foot, then how did she get here so soon after me? This girl was an enigma all around.

"Incidentally, I don't have any business with you either, Chee-chee."

"Oh...okay..."

What a weirdo. But...maybe if I ask her for advice, she could help me. Surely, she and Hino kiss each other on the forehead, right? Don't they seem like the type? I didn't have anyone better to ask, so I decided to take this as a sign from God or whoever. I pointed down at the magazine I was holding.

"So, totally unrelated to this," I began, though it was possible my disclaimer only made it even more obvious.

"Totally unrelated. Got it."

Did she really believe me that easily? At least, it *sounded* like she believed me... I couldn't really tell from her expression. She was hard to read, kind of like Shimamura was, but not quite.

"Yeah, totally unrelated, but uh..."

"It's about Shimamura, right?"

I didn't get that far yet!

"I was wondering, you know, what sort of location might...put Shimamura in the mood to do a favor for me..." How could I explain it to her without going into detail? This conversation was so roundabout, I might as well have taken a detour to Russia. My panic dripped down my body in the form of a cold sweat.

"Ah, I get it. So it's a competition."

"What? A competition? Why would you think that?"

I had barely explained anything, and yet she seemed to instantly understand. In her own mind, at least. "I'm sure of it," she declared firmly.

Where did she get this unwavering confidence when she almost certainly didn't know the whole story? She wasn't just being stubborn either. My only conclusion was that she hadn't put a single ounce of thought into it.

"And if you win, then you get to ask Shimamura for a favor, right? I understand completely." She nodded so absently, I was convinced she wasn't listening anymore.

"No, it's not a competition—well, okay. Maybe it *could* be...?"

"It can be! Don't worry!"

About what? Granted, it seemed like this would steer the conversation in the direction I wanted, but...how did she arrive at "a competition," anyway?

"If you want to defeat Shimamura, then I have a suggestion."

"Uh...okay...?"

"Make it a boomerang-throwing competition."

At first, I wasn't sure I heard her correctly. *Boomerang-throwing competition?* "...Why?"

"I doubt she's been practicing, so if you train up a little, you can beat her."

"Beat her...with the boomerang?"

"Good girls don't hit their friends with boomerangs," she scolded me, swinging her arms in an alternating pattern. "Oh, but I guess you're not a good girl, huh? I forgot."

"No, I...I quit being a delinquent." Not that I ever set out to be one in the first place.

"In that case, you can't hit people. Now, there are a few different ways to compete with boomerangs—"

"I don't need you to explain it. I'm not doing it."

"First things first, let's go buy you a boomerang of your own." She grabbed me by the shoulder and started to drag me off.

"Wait a minute, wait a minute!" I resisted until she stopped. "For the record...I *do* technically own a boomerang." Shimamura had given me one as a Christmas present. But I only ever used it as a decoration on my shelf.

"Really?" She looked at me, her eyes sparkling. "Do you play?"

"Not at all." I shook my head.

"Oh, okay." Her gaze wandered from left to right, and after a beat, she seemingly forgot everything I said. "If you want to beat Shimamura, boomerang throwing is your best bet! I'll even coach you myself!"

"What? You'll coach me?"

"Well, you wanna win, right? Then you need some coaching! Yup!"

Where did *that* come from? I was still so full of questions, and yet Nagafuji seemed to have it all worked out.

"Now then, Chee-chee, we'd better get started!"

"Huh? Oh...uh...okay...?"

"Go drop your stuff off at home. You know the park that's right around the corner? Yeah? Perfect! Let's both grab our boomerangs and meet back up over there!"

Something about this didn't feel right, but Nagafuji clearly wasn't taking no for an answer. As I grappled with my total inability to assert boundaries, the two of us briefly parted ways, leaving me alone with my misgivings.

A boomerang date? Seriously?

Additionally, the fact that she called me "Chee-chee" the entire time suggested that she had once again forgotten what my name was.

"Glad you could make it, Chee-chee!"

Yep. She's completely forgotten my actual name.

I was still wearing my school uniform, but Nagafuji had changed clothes. She was now wearing a shirt that read INSTRUCTOR. I decided not to comment on it.

This park was located next to the shopping mall (assuming it was big enough to count as one) and we were the only two people out here. Partly because it was a weekday, but also, kids just didn't seem to play in parks much these days. Sign of the times.

All that aside—I really never imagined I'd ever use this thing as anything more than a decoration. When I showed it to her, she murmured approvingly, tweaking its arms. But after a moment she paused and tilted her head.

"Huh? Wait a minute... Is this...?"

"Something wrong with it?"

"Nah, it's no big deal. Now, then, time to tune it up!"

I stood there and watched as she twisted its arms back and forth, making minute adjustments. "Um...thanks for helping me," I muttered shyly, shoulders hunched.

Scoffing, she thrust out her ample chest and flat tummy, and I quickly realized what she was getting at.

"Thanks for helping me...Instructor," I corrected myself.

"Heh heh heh."

Apparently, she liked it. Was *that* the whole reason she was helping me? To get me to call her Instructor? As for her boomerang, there were holes in each of its three arms.

"There you go! It's been fine-tuned for maximum aerodynamic lift," she explained.

"Whoa." That sounded hardcore. Not that I had any interest in becoming a boomerang athlete or whatever.

"Now, the trick is to hold it gently, flick it lightly, and try to give it a lot of spins."

"Hmm."

"It's all about the spins!"

"......"

"Sorry, I've just always wanted to say that."

"Oookay, then."

"Basically, you want to aim for a logarithmic spiral with the golden ratio—eh, whatever. The most important part is, throw it vertically," she explained as she handed my "fine-tuned" boomerang back to me. It felt like I'd heard it all before somewhere.

The park was separated from the river by a single unpaved trail, and the only shelter was a single patio umbrella in the rest area. Needless to say, it was a safe place to throw a boomerang or two.

"If you don't throw it correctly, you could really hurt yourself, so be sure to focus."

"Got it." As instructed, I held it vertically in my left hand.

"It's the world's first girls' boomerang light novel!"

Are you going to let me focus or not?

"Wait, what? Chee-chee, are you left-handed?" she asked suddenly.

"Yeah."

"In that case, I actually gotta tune it the other way around. Lemme borrow it again."

I handed it back to her, and she switched the direction of the arms.

"Hmmm..."

Admittedly, I didn't understand much about Nagafuji, but she sincerely seemed to want more people to throw boomerangs with her. Maybe Hino refused to play with her...? Evidently, there were some things that even the best of friends couldn't share together. In that case, I was likely going to have my work cut out for me trying to share every little thing with Shimamura.

"Which way is the wind blowing...? This way. Okay, throw it this way."

With the re-tuning complete, she returned my boomerang. Then she tested the wind, and once she was sure, she pointed in the direction she wanted me to throw. *This boomerang stuff sure is complicated. I thought you just kinda threw it and that's it.*

"Remember, it's not about force. The spins are what make it fly."

There she goes, babbling about something again.

I made my throw without too much effort. The lightweight boomerang quickly left my hand, and I was startled to see just how high it flew. It sliced diagonally through the air, did a little lap around the park, then arced back toward me. *How does it know to come back anyway? So odd,* I thought idly to myself.

But although it was headed in my direction, it was a considerable distance off the mark. I followed it with my eyes as I ran sideways, then reached out and clapped it between my palms just in time. I must have looked pretty stupid practically diving for it, but whatever. *Good enough, right?*

When I walked back over with the boomerang, Nagafuji nodded in satisfaction. "No complaints!"

"Huh?"

"My little baby bird's already leaving the nest..."

She smiled wistfully at me like I was her disciple. *I thought this was going to be a serious training session, not Boomerang 101! We've only been out here, like, ten minutes!*

"Oh, but if I were to offer some advice..." Using her finger, she drew a circle in the dirt around me approximately twelve feet in diameter. "Try to practice until you can catch it without leaving this circle!"

"Is that how it's supposed to be played?"

"Yup!" she nodded. "Then you and Shimamura compete to see how many times you can catch it inside the playing field. The pros only count how many times they can catch it *in a row*, but eh, that doesn't really matter as long as you win."

"Oh. Right." *Why is she so dead set on this boomerang competition? Ugh, I picked the wrong person to ask for advice.* But then again, it wasn't like I had any other ideas.

"This concludes our coaching session. Unfortunately, tomorrow I'll be very busy entertaining Hino."

"Oh. Okay." *Sounds like a valid reason to me.*

"May victory be yours!" And with that, she ran off on foot.

Come to think of it, I seemed to recall that Nagafuji didn't know how to ride a bike. Hence she always mooched rides from Hino. *Lucky... I wish Shimamura would give me rides around town...* But of course, it was far too late to pretend like I didn't know how to ride my own bike.

With that thought, I headed over the little bridge that passed over the river...

"Nice work out there," a voice called out of nowhere, and I whipped my head up in alarm. It was Shimamura.

"Wha?! Sh-Shimamura...?" *What is she doing here?!*

"Hm? Oh, I saw you and Nagafuji walking along together just now."

"Oh...right. I-I see... Interesting..."

I was shocked. Shimamura was dressed in her street clothes, suggesting she was on her way home from an outing somewhere. But she didn't seem to have seen what Nagafuji and I were up to at the park.

"I'm surprised—you don't often hang out with Nagafuji, do you?"

"Yeah, uh, not often."

She gazed at me for a long moment, and then...

"Well, just so you know, Adachi..." She walked up beside me and whispered in my ear: "You're not allowed to cheat on me."

I heard a *whssshhh* as all the blood drained from my face. Then, as she straightened up, I could see her lips curl in a most delighted smirk.

"If you're going to set ground rules for me, then I expect you to follow them yourself, too. Otherwise it's no fair."

"Wh... No! That—I wasn't—you're my one and only!"

"Methinks the lady doth protest too much... Just kidding!"

As she giggled at my panic, I chased after her, desperate to explain myself.

Every now and then, I stopped to picture what life would be like if I'd never met Shimamura. I probably would have spent today like any other weekend—sitting in my room and watching the clock, unsure if I wanted it to go faster or slower. Now and then I would ask myself: What if I had never developed this ardent passion? Without it, I probably could have come to accept the target of my affection turning their attention elsewhere. I would have convinced myself that it just wasn't meant to be.

But instead, this is where I ended up.

Her voice made my heart flutter. The thought of her filled me with a burning heat that gnawed at my insides.

I was stricken with impatience and frustration, but at the same time, I felt optimistic that I could fight through it. Hesitation, resentment, and other esoteric riddles forced me to confront the outside world. All of this was caused by Shimamura. She was my everything.

And so Sunday rolled around—the day of our date.

My body ached from sleep deprivation, but this always happened whenever I agreed to meet up with Shimamura on a weekend, so I was getting used to it. Before now, the two of us had only ever "hung out," but today we were "going on a date." Anyone would be nervous in my shoes. My skin and eyes were so dry, I could practically hear the sand rustling. Was I forgetting to blink again?

Rows of cirrocumulus clouds lined the mackerel sky—yet another sign that autumn was on its way. It was in the lingering heat of autumn that Shimamura and I first met, and this year, autumn would see our relationship continue to evolve. So what did *next* autumn have in store for us? I couldn't even begin to imagine.

That being said...was it the right choice to spend all my date prep time throwing my boomerang around? Or had Nagafuji steered me in the wrong direction? She almost certainly had, but only the boomerang tucked in my bookbag knew for sure.

We had agreed to meet up in front of a moderately tacky sports gym—the one I visited with Shimamura a while back—but when I first told her, she didn't sound too enthused about it over the phone. "Oh. Hmm. Nah, it's fine, but... Well, whatever," she had said. This was very concerning to me.

Then, before long, she arrived, bookbag slung over her shoulder. "Yoo-hoo!"

"Wow..."

When I paused to take a good look at her, it quickly became apparent that she was adorable from head to toe. Her shoulders, legs, hips—her clothes did nothing to conceal how perfect they were. Even the soles of her shoes were cute...uh...probably. *God, I'm such a terminal case.*

"Good m—"

But before I could finish saying hi, she suddenly leaned in close.

"Wh-what is it?"

She was standing on tiptoe, examining my forehead up close. Was the big moment already here?! My fingers quivered.

"Oh. Disappointing." She lowered herself back down again.

"Wh-what is?"

"I half-expected you to smear honey up there or some-thing."

I promptly started choking.

"Oh, no! Adachi, are you coming down with something?"

"I'm fine," I insisted, waving a hand dismissively. But for the record, I decided to ask: "Wh-what if I *did* have honey smeared on my forehead...?"

"I would have told you to go wash it off. So where are you taking me? The gym?"

"This way."

We crossed two streets, turned the corner, and quickly arrived at the municipal athletic field. Fortunately, there were no clubs or corporate sports teams scheduled to practice today, so the place was empty, save for some kids playing catch over in the corner.

"You're not gonna invite me to play one-on-one soccer or something, are you?" Shimamura asked skeptically.

Was it just me, or did I detect a hint of nostalgia in her voice and gaze? Maybe it was a game she used to play with someone a long time ago. Her younger sister? Or that girl I didn't know? The thought made me grit my teeth.

"Here." I pulled the boomerang out of my bookbag and hesitantly held it out. Her eyes widened ever so slightly.

"Oh, *now* I get it."

"Get what...?"

"I think I know where you got your inspiration for this, that's all. So you wanted to throw it around and relive our childhoods?"

"I wanted to...have a competition...and if I win..." *Mumble, mumble.*

She looked at the boomerang in my hand. "A competition," she repeated carefully. Then she smirked in understanding. "Adachi, you little cheat! I bet you got a ton of practice in beforehand, didn't you?"

I started to choke again. Unsurprisingly, she had seen right through me. Now what? If she refused, it would mean I'd wasted the entire past week leading up to this!

"You really put effort into this. I'm proud."

...Wait, what? She's proud of me?

"Okay, then! If you can make a good throw *and* catch it afterward, I guess I could be convinced." With that, she sat down on a nearby bench.

...Wait, what? That's it? Is she being nice and making it easy for me? No, that can't be it. She's not like that,

I cautioned myself. Shimamura's idea of "being nice" was ever so slightly different.

"You only get one shot at it, okay?" She snickered cruelly.

See what I mean?! One shot! I had grasped the basics during practice, but I wasn't 100 percent confident. There was a chance I could screw up.

"It's not like if I mess up, you'll never kiss my forehead ever again…right?"

"I don't knoooow…" She smirked widely. *Is it just me, or has she been smiling more often lately?* Normally, it was charming, but right now, she was being downright mean.

I wiped my palms off on my clothes, then stared straight ahead. I couldn't afford to slip up. As my heart raced and my body tensed up, I eased into my throwing stance and braced myself. My palms were already sweaty again, and now the boomerang was sweaty too. My instructor's voice echoed in my ears: *Focus. Remember to breathe. Remember to relax. It's all in the spins.*

It was kind of distracting, actually.

I prayed for my boomerang to fly high. Then my knees stiffened as I shifted my weight…and took the shot.

Go, go, go!

The boomerang soared. Now I just needed to catch it.

Calmly, carefully, I followed its trajectory with my eyes. But then the boomerang—and the scenery around it—began to warp. I was so nervous, my field of vision was narrowing, and I was getting distracted by the sound of my own heavy breathing.

Get it together! This is the moment of truth! As I psyched myself up, I kept watching the boomerang. Nothing else mattered; I didn't even care if there was a meteor crashing to Earth right on top of me. My vision had turned red, but I didn't care about that either. I focused only on the most important point. That was how I lived my life.

The boomerang arced back toward me. My throw had met the basic prerequisite. Now came the hard part.

There! I dashed sideways in tandem with the boomerang. Then I reached out to secure my future, just like that one guy with the seeds from *Fist of the North Star*. My body stretched—my arms stretched—and then—

Clap!

Shimamura...caught...the boomerang...from the bench.

"...Oh, sorry! It was right in front of me, so my reflexes kinda kicked in..."

The sweat on my back trickled down all at once in a single shudder. Her gaze darted to and fro as she fiddled with the boomerang's arms.

"It was, uhhh...you know...a group effort! Love and teamwork!"

"Uh...y-yeah...that. Totally." *Does this count, though? Does it count or what?!* The sweat that dripped from my nose was burning hot and threatening to evaporate.

"So is this the end of the date?" she asked.

"Uhhhhh...well..."

And so it was revealed: I was so focused on my short-term objective, I had completely forgotten to plan anything else.

"You may not have much in the way of forethought, but I don't mind."

She noticed my silence and glossed over it, smiling awkwardly. But "I don't mind" was decidedly *not* the same as "I like it," so I shrank into myself.

"Well, let's see... First, we should eat something, since it's lunchtime and all," she continued, without checking the time whatsoever. She was the one who picked our meetup time; could she have anticipated that my "date plans" would end quickly? I couldn't help but interpret this as a kind gesture, and it warmed my heart.

"Should I go buy us something? Or would you rather go to a sit-down place? Oh, um, it'll be my treat. I mean, I have plenty of money, so yeah..." My savings account was still quite robust, since I had nothing to spend it on.

"Now hold on, Adachi. You don't think I'm some kind of *gold digger*, do you?" She frowned as if mortally offended.

Suppressing the impulse to correct the record, I instead opted for a more playful response and recoiled melodramatically. "Wait...y-you're not?!"

"Oh, I most certainly am."

"Wha?!" I was joking, but she totally called my bluff. I froze.

"Just kidding. Anyway, turns out you're loaded, huh? *Interesting.*" I could practically feel her gaze trailing over my jaw and temples, and it tickled. "You're pretty, and you're rich, and...uhhh...pretty..."

"What?"

"Yep, you're a keeper! I've got such good taste!" She laughed so widely, I could see the backsides of her teeth.

"Ha ha...ha...ha ha..." Awkwardly, I forced myself to laugh along with her. It felt like she was saying my only good points were my looks and my money, but it gave me warm fuzzies all the same.

"And here, you used to send me to fetch your lunch for you back when we first met..."

"Huh?!"

"Anyway, no, you don't have to go buy anything."

"...Huh?" I froze mid-jog, facing the exit. She dug through her bookbag, then raised something over her head.

"Ta-daaa! I packed a lunch for us! Just like I promised!" She offered me a smile and a sandwich covered in cling wrap.

"Oh..."

Overcome with emotion, my words idled in my throat and refused to come out. Weakly, I staggered to the bench and collapsed down onto it.

"It's nothing fancy, though. I only know how to make, like, basic stuff."

She giggled casually in an attempt to play it off. It worked, of course. As she unwrapped the sandwiches, they seemed to light up with all the colors of the rainbow.

"Wow...!"

"Here you goooo!"

She handed me an egg salad sandwich; I started to take it, but then realized she was holding it up to my mouth. *Oh, I get it.* I leaned forward and took a bite.

"How is it?"

The back of my throat burned hot. The flavor was...honestly kind of bland. "It's...it's really...super-duper good!"

"Ha ha! You're such a bad liar."

She saw through me instantly. Nevertheless, I opened my mouth again and prompted her for more.

"Heh. Well, it's still nice to hear, even if you're just being polite."

Pleased, she held out the rest of the sandwich. Unfortunately, I chose that exact moment to lean forward, and as a result, she inadvertently stuffed it down my throat.

"Mmffg!" Half-choking, I struggled to avoid showing any outward discomfort as I chewed. Then, as I swallowed, I stared down at the ground. "Hey, um... Shimamura? Can I ask you something?"

"What might that be?"

I figured I should probably ask while she was in a good mood...or would it ruin the moment completely? Unable to decide, I ultimately asked the question that had plagued my mind for an eternity:

"That, uh, girl you were with at that other festival that happened a while ago—who is she?" Realizing I was rambling, I took a breath, and added, "Just wondering." I started to hang my head, but caught myself and forced myself to look at her.

Her smile was in the process of fading, but she

answered nonetheless. "An old friend," she sighed. "She invited me to go, so I said yes."

An "old friend"? As in, before you knew me? You never mentioned anything about an old friend before. This is the first I've heard about her. Why keep it a secret? You didn't feel like you needed to tell me? But I'm your girlfriend! Maybe I wasn't always, but I am now, so...so...!

I could feel my face starting to crumple, and if that happened, I was sure to start crying. And *that* would ruin everything. My meager few months of experience with Shimamura cautioned me to rein myself in. I took a deep breath to get my voice and emotions under control. Then, once I had regained a modicum of composure...

"From now on...can you only do that stuff with...with me?" Timidly, I peered at her.

"Hmmm..." She smiled awkwardly as her gaze wandered. "I swear, you're such a little handful."

She stroked my hair like she was tickling the ivories of a piano; at first, her fingers flinched back, but then her caress deepened. *Grrrr...* Biting back my frustration, I decided to address the remaining elephant in the room—

"What are you pouting about now?"

Evidently, my displeasure had shown itself on my face.

"Shimamura...you always treat me like a little kid."

"Do I?" She didn't seem aware that she was doing it; she withdrew her hand and gazed down at her palm. "Well, whenever I look at you, I feel...protective? I guess?"

"I don't like it." I knew she was just trying to be affectionate, but an inexplicable sense of aversion took precedence inside me. At least for now, I was craving something different.

Pinching her lower lip between her fingers, Shimamura gazed at me pensively. "Okay, then. How should I treat you?"

There was a hint of playfulness in her tone, as if she knew the answer and had chosen to ask anyway. I shot her a look that said, "Do I have to spell it out?" She returned it with a smile that said "Yes. Yes, you do."

Uggghhh.

"Like a...g-girlfriend..."

"Oho, I see. Like a *girlfriend*." She rose to her feet and walked in front of me. Then she put her hands on my shoulders, blocking out the sun. "Like this?"

Reflexively, I swallowed the last traces of the sandwich. "Yeah...like that..."

My shoulders started to ache; my throat was tight, and my stomach felt constricted.

"Do it s-slow, okay?"

This time, I wanted to watch every last moment and sear it into my eyelids.

"Slow? Okay, then, nice and slow..."

She leaned in, one agonizing centimeter at a time. So slow, in fact, I thought she might go for my lips instead. My fingers wriggled like worms against the bench. Then she combed my bangs up and pressed her lips firmly against my forehead.

The blood throbbed in my veins in a single coagulated mass. Deep down, I thought I heard a voice— a mysterious voice far deeper than my own—singing "Hallelujah!" over and over. My vision blurred. Then, gradually, Shimamura's outline reappeared, as if she had surfaced from the depths of the water.

"Is that what you wanted? Gosh, this is so embarrassing..."

Scratching her cheek, she started to pull away—but I grabbed her hand. Then I looked up, directly into her eyes, and told her everything that was in my heart.

"I love you."

"Mm-hmm."

"I'm crazy about you."

"Mm-hmm."

"Stay with me forever."

"...Okay."

Though I tried to think of the perfect words, I could only manage to string together a bunch of worn-out clichés. But in the end, my girlfriend accepted each and every one of them with a smile.

interlude Yachi Comes Calling

ON MY WAY HOME, I spot a familiar figure with her back turned, so I jog after her. You'd think maybe it was raining, because a tiny bit of running is all it takes to make my clothes feel damp. But no. While summer break's almost over, summer itself is still going strong.

"Yoo-hoo!"

I give her a little shove from behind. Her cheeks are puffed out like she's eating something. Then, finally, she turns. "Mmm?"

"What the?"

The Yachi I'm looking at isn't quite the same Yachi. Whaaa?

"What. Do. You. Want?" She speaks in a weird robotic voice and raises both hands menacingly. Meanwhile, she's still chewing something.

"Oh, nothing... Hmmm..."

From the front, they look nothing alike—their eye colors, hair colors, and hair lengths are totally different. And their faces are different too. Also, this one's shorter. So why did I ever mistake her for Yachi? Now I'm confused.

The only thing they have in common is that their hair sparkles. But unlike Yachi's sky blue, this girl's sparklies are silver, like the winter snow came early. It's *mystical*.

"I thought you were a friend of mine. Sorry."

For some reason, she looked like Yachi when her back was turned...but why?

"Oh. Well, then."

With a shrug, Not-Yachi starts to walk off. Hmmm... I guess she doesn't care? But just then, she turns around and walks back. When I gaze into her dark blue eyes, it feels like I'm peering into the depths of the ocean.

"Why did you think that?" she asks after a *long* delay. This girl seems to process things at her own pace. What an odd duck.

"Well, when I saw you from behind, you looked a lot like her. Identical, actually."

"*Identical*?"

Tilting her head, she starts to count on her fingers...

over and over and over. I don't know what she's counting, but it kinda reminds me of Yachi.

"No, it just doesn't fit. You must have *terrible* eyesight."

"Huh?"

"But it reminded me of something I was trying to remember. Thanks for the help. Now, I bid you adieu!" With an energetic wave, she runs off. "I think it was this way...?" she murmurs to herself before making a right turn around the corner, leaving a trail of silver sparklies in her wake more fleeting than the summer sun in September.

"...Uhhhh..."

Who the heck *was* she? Because she just ran off in the direction of the graveyard.

"Now...there is nowhere left for me on this earth."

Yachi's lying in the corner of the room, reading my sister's manga out loud and doing all the character voices. She does this with every book she reads. One time I asked her why, and she said, "It's easier to read this way."

Yachi doesn't let anything stop her. She's hard to grasp, like a cloud of smoke. This morning I woke up, and as usual, she was already here, lounging around. But I don't know where she comes from or where she goes when she leaves.

"I don't quite follow the plot, but nevertheless, this is a fitting tool with which to practice Earthling language." Once she's finished with the book, she sets it down and crawls over to me on her hands and knees. "Little, have you finished your homework?"

"Mmm...I still have a little more."

It's messed up that they give us tons of homework every time we get a couple days off from school. The weekend doesn't feel like a weekend at all.

"Alas."

Yachi crawls back to the corner. Then she flops back down and grabs the next volume of manga. I guess she really doesn't go to school...but why not? Part of me is jealous that she never has to do homework, but another part of me is worried about her future. What if she turns into a delinquent like my sister? Then again, if she's not going to school, I guess she already is one.

I look over my shoulder at her. As she lays on her side, her hair pools on the floor. The strands themselves are bright blue, but the sparklies make it look a bit more pastel, like the furthest reaches of a cloudless sky. By this point, I'm kinda used to it, but every now and then I'll stop and realize: gosh, her hair is such a crazy color.

For a while I gaze at it, entranced. Then she notices me, sits up, and giggles. "I see what you're after, Little."

"Huh?"

"I should have known you'd spot these rice crackers." She pulls a package of crackers out from under her clothes. I didn't actually spot them, though. "I'm impressed to see that you've mastered the fine art of staring."

"Wait...I was staring?"

"Yes, and for quite a long time."

Was it really that long? I feel kinda embarrassed for some reason. I wanna say it's not true, but then I see how much progress I've made on my homework (not much) and realize that it probably *is* true.

"Now, then, you may have some." She opens the package and offers it to me, so I decide to take a little snack break and walk away from my desk.

Oddly enough, even though the crackers were hidden under her clothes while she was lying down, they're not crushed at all. Every now and then, she defies my expectations. Or is it the crackers? Are the crackers weird somehow? I bite into one as a test. The faintly sweet and salty taste of soy sauce dances on my tongue.

"Yum yum!"

Yachi seems to enjoy them about ten times more than I do. The sparkle of her smile is on a whole different level. When I look at her, something in my chest gets all floaty. Like water, but warmer.

"The other day, I saw a girl and thought it was you."

"Mmm?" Her eyes dart over to me, shining with other-worldly color.

"She didn't really look like you at all, but for some reason, she seemed just like you..."

"A clone of me? Yes, I imagine there is at least one of those in this world." She kept on crunching her crackers. "I copied my face from a different individual, so I do have one identical twin."

"Oh...really?"

"Yes." She swallows her food.

I don't know how she "copied her face," but it sounds crazy. Or is she just joking? I watch her for a moment, but she just seems perfectly content, like always. So if I had to guess, she's probably...

"Yachi, are you really an alien?"

"Of course!" she declares. But after a moment, she falters. Her eyes dart around and around. Then her lips curl into a big, smug smirk. "But in actuality, I am not."

"Wait...you're not?"

"I am an adolescent like any other."

"*Adolescent*...?" I don't know what that word means, but I do know that Yachi is *not at all* like any other kid.

"Well, there you have it."

She stashes her crackers, then flops back down onto the floor. What was *that* about? Does she want to keep it a secret? I think it's a little late for that... Even after I go back to my desk, I keep glancing over my shoulder at her. Her hair and eyes seem to ripple with white-crested waves.

Then she peers at me from behind her manga. "There will be no more rice crackers for you today, Little."

"Oh...okay." Hastily, I turn around and face forward.

"But perhaps tomorrow."

Then I hear her little feet thumping down the hall. Maybe she's in a big rush to get to tomorrow... Classic Yachi. I'll see you then.

If we had enrolled at different schools...if the gym didn't have a loft...if I was just a bit more responsible... would something still have blossomed between me and Adachi?

To me, the inner workings of destiny were truly, deeply fascinating.

4. A Tiny Prayer

GIVEN HOW MUCH I liked to sleep, I probably experienced more dreams than the average person. Would this prove useful to me in any way? I didn't have the answer to that. But in order to find it, I would need... to go back to sleep.

Zzzzz.

I forget who it was, but someone once said that dreams are adventures that take place in the dark of night. Indeed, only during the night am I spared the judgmental voice scoffing at me for sleeping. Night is when my heart can truly roam free—a dark, endless expanse, but every now and then, I catch a glimpse of light. These tiny twinkling lights are what people call "memories." Without them, the darkness would overtake our hearts, pinning us in place.

In the darkness, someone calls to me: *Shima-chaaaan!* I turn around, only to be met with the clear blue sky.

If you wish for it, your dreams can always be bright. They're packed with fresh memories, after all.

A much younger Tarumi comes running up to me— and right past me. Ahead, I can see a younger version of myself, but I can only vaguely remember her. Back then, I didn't think too much about keeping up appearances; no, I was more interested in everything else around me.

Is this what it was like back then? I chase after them, but I don't need to run. A few quick strides is all it takes to catch up. Then it hits home just how *small* they are. Was it ever frustrating to have such stumpy little arms and legs? Was everything I wanted still within my reach?

We're walking down a street not too far from my house. There are no cars, and upon further inspection, the buildings all match how they look in the present day rather than an accurate reflection of how they used to be. The only difference is that the sky overhead is pure blue. Experimentally, I reach out to it. Nope, it's just as untouchable as it's always been.

Taru-chan! Ghshsh!

Little Me is making some kind of weird noise... Is that supposed to be a giggle?

Shima-chan! Ha ha ha ha ha!

Tarumi starts cackling like something is hilarious. Then I remember all the conversations we used to have that were just like this one. Somehow, we understood each other perfectly through our laughter alone. At least, that was what it felt like.

When I'm awake, I can scarcely remember what Tarumi used to be like as a kid, so I only ever see her in my dreams. Little Tarumi always has a runny nose, so she looks pretty derpy—but if I mentioned it to present-day Tarumi, she'd probably deny that she ever looked like this. Not that I've seen her in a while... Come to think of it, I haven't heard her voice since the last time I hung up on her.

Drawn together, pulled apart. Approached and pushed away. Will the two of us fall out of contact again? If we do, then I guess that's life. After all, if I hang out with her in secret and Adachi finds out, she'll get hurt.

These days Adachi's really settled into her role as my girlfriend. But what about me? Am I going to be able to handle it? I've been giving her a reasonable amount of what she wants, so I think I'm probably fine. But every now and then, her feelings for me feel intense to a frightening degree, and I'm just not sure I can reciprocate. I'm not starved for love like she is—I've already experienced it with other people in a variety of ways.

Shima-chan, where are you going today?

"Good question."

Umm, I'm going to play on the field at school.

"Oh, yeah... I sure did that a lot."

Tarumi and I would always go to the local elementary school, stand in the field, and play catch. There wasn't a lot of crime back in those days, so we were allowed on the premises on weekends, even though we weren't students there. And I *loved* to play catch. Frankly, I'm lucky Tarumi tolerated it as much as she did. I guess she really cared about me...not to toot my own horn or anything.

But I won't be able to stay with Taru-chan forever.

Little Me looks over her shoulder at me.

Then Tarumi turns back, her bright smile gone, and says in a flat voice: *Yeah, I know. Once you find a new friend, you'll throw me away.*

She's as cold as the spring water I once touched at a tourist attraction somewhere. I feel like I've been frozen solid in the middle of summer. Without any trace of emotion, her youthful face is flawless and robotic.

"*Throw you away*? Is that how it felt?" Smiling evasively, I tilt my head at this phantom visited upon me by my guilty conscience.

Interpersonal relationships aren't a one-way street. If people didn't always make me carry the whole thing on my shoulders, then maybe I wouldn't keep accidentally dropping it. Do they really think I know how to juggle? Me, the same idiot who always ran around slamming face-first into walls?

It's sad, but true, Little Me answers unprompted. *But it's okay, Taru-chan. As a kid, I can stay with you forever.*

Forever?

Yup, forever. 'Cuz we'll always be little kids. Then, Little Me takes Tarumi by the hand, and Tarumi sniffles happily. How very philosophical of you, Little Me.

So how does this work, exactly? The parts from my old memories make sense, but what about Tarumi's anachronistic comment just now? Where did it come from? If this was a dream, then my brain must have penned the script, but I can't find it anywhere. So who created this dream?

I look up at the sky. Is someone else out there, beyond the veil, spying on my memories?

But as I gaze upward, my consciousness gradually rises to the surface.

So ended the, uh, "dream" I had. As I suspected, if I immersed myself fully, I could watch a little longer. But the reason I couldn't confidently declare my dreams "illusions" was because of the way they sometimes showed me my past. I refused to believe I was hallucinating all that time.

The room was still dark, and I was drowsy, so it was unusual for me to wake up partway through. I lay back down and attempted to go back to sleep.

Zzzzz.

Yep, it worked.

I return to what looks like the same street, as if un-pausing a movie I was in the middle of watching.

"But if this is a movie, then I doubt it's a good one."

From an outside perspective, I'm just walking down the street, uninterested in anyone who passes me by. I can only imagine how dreary it must look. Little Tarumi and Little Me are both nowhere to be found; they must have faded away into the background, hand in hand, like good friends.

My memories safely retain all the things that no longer exist in reality.

I've sensed for a while now that my friendship with Tarumi just isn't going to work out. After everything it took to bring us back together—to restore our bond—now it's all falling apart again. Even a blind idiot like me can see that much. If I want to keep it, then I need to take action, fast. But there's an invisible force holding me back.

Adachi. Adachi is the problem. Adachi has single-handedly destroyed one of my personal relationships. When I think about it logically, it's insane. She just kicks the door down, tramples all over my feelings and my life, and tries to make me play by her rules. She's not fair to anyone, least of all me, and it's this bias that fills her with red-hot passion and spurs her on. To me, this raw intensity is enviable, exasperating, and endearing, all at the same time. I know it's contradictory, but it's the honest truth.

These things we call "emotions" are rarely ever consistent. They're *supposed* to be complicated and mysterious and all that. But Adachi isn't contradictory in the least. She cares about one thing and one thing only; her emotions are unpolished and unfiltered. Maybe that, if anything, was what drew me to her.

A white shadow shoots past my feet, as if the wind itself has taken form. As I watch him go, his wagging tail seems to brush against my eyes. It's Gon, fully grown, but with all the energy of his puppy days—the best of both worlds. The distance grows between us as he dashes off.

"Heh heh heh. You sure are feisty today."

He's big, strong, and healthy. Dreams sure are great, aren't they? I find myself torn between the urge to chase after him and the urge to cry my eyes out; after a bit of waffling back and forth, I decide to do both at the same time. Not like anyone else is here to see it. This place belongs to me alone, and I'm allowed to cry in private. Especially since I'll probably forget it happened once I wake up.

So I run as fast as I can. My body feels weightless, like I left my lungs behind, but since I don't need to breathe, it's hard to tell if I'm making any progress. No matter how hard I run, I never seem to move forward. The distance between myself and Gon never gets any smaller. One would think I would run out of road eventually, but that never seems to happen.

But that's okay. I don't mind if I can never catch up.

The scenery swirls around me in a vortex and starts to fade away. Along with Gon, the city skyline burns into pale, pointed shapes. Even the ground beneath me starts to curl in on itself, like a sheet of notebook paper slowly being crumpled into a ball. I can no longer chase after Gon. He's disappearing, and so am I.

But I don't want either of us to vanish. I don't want to go anywhere at all.

The next time I awoke, I could see the faint gray light of daybreak streaming in through the gaps in the curtains. Soon, a new day would begin. I could always get dressed, go for a jog, and wait for the rest of my family to rise, but... *mehhh.* I rolled over. My eyes and cheeks felt warm and damp—soaked in the tears from a good yawn, perhaps.

I guess it probably won't work this time...

I zoned out for a while. Then my eyelids slowly drooped.

Zzzzz.

As it turned out, I had underestimated myself.

This time, no one is waiting for me when I arrive.

"Guess I'm all alone."

Story of my life.

Sure is ridiculous just how much I can sleep, I think to myself with a sigh as I look upward. If I sleep for thirteen hours of the day, does that make sleeping my default state? That would mean my dreams *are* my reality...and in turn, I would be freed from all the worst parts of the waking world, which would be awesome. Just one problem, though: in the dream world, I can't sleep. I'll lose my favorite pastime.

But enough about that.

I find myself enshrouded in darkness so dense, even the light of dawn can't penetrate it. I can't see my own hands waving in front of my face. I'm not even sure I have a body anymore. I turn my head and look around, but can't see a single light source. This is a dream without any memories.

So I start walking aimlessly. My footsteps sound so distant, it's hard to say if I'm even walking on solid ground. Kinda feels like my feet are sinking, or at least, the scenery sorta seems to be shifting up and down... Am I even moving forward?

If I had to guess, I'd say this is probably what Adachi's dreams are like, since she doesn't seem to have many happy memories. Or maybe her dreams are just a slideshow of still images of me... Honestly, the idea creeps me out, but she'd probably love it. That's the kind of world she wants to be in.

As far as Adachi is concerned, I'm the only person she needs in her life—just me and her, forever. But if she asked me to go to the ends of the earth with her, I would say no. If she demanded that we create a world all our own, I would refuse. I mean, at that point, I might as well just be alone, right? That way I can be free from any and all hassle.

I'm only spending my life with Adachi if it's in a world full of people. If it was just the two of us, our life would be as bleak as this dream.

But while it's a pretty stark contrast from those other dreams, it's still a piece of my heart all the same. It's like the chill that follows a gust of warm air. Whenever I'm having fun, I can feel it waiting right around the corner; whenever things are going well, I start obsessing over the moment it all breaks down. The darkness produced by this state of mind keeps my memories at bay.

Time dilutes these old memories like water. This alone is inevitable. If you want to hold onto them, you have to keep them fresh—but if you condense them too much, they'll lose what made them special to begin with.

Are my memories still pure? God only knows how murky they've gotten.

Then I see a round, pale light floating absently in the middle of nowhere. Curious, I approach it. It's a familiar head of blue hair.

"How much longer until breakfast...?"

"Is that all you ever care about?"

"Oh! G'day, Shimamura-san!" Yashiro turns to face me. What's with the bad Aussie accent? "Shima-moo-ra, Shima-moo-ra..."

"I'm not a cow. Anyway, how the heck did you waltz in here?" This is *my* dream, and no, I'm not going to make you breakfast.

"It was easy." She flaps her arms up and down. Thanks to her faintly glowing hair, I can see her expression and everything. "Are you still sleepy?"

So she's fully aware that this is a dream. What a weirdo. "Yeah, just a little."

"In that case, I shall accompany you."

She toddles up beside me, casting her dim light onto me, and it feels like I've gained a lantern on my quest. Now I can almost see my feet and actually hear my footsteps.

"Hmmm..." For some reason, this all feels a little too... crisp? For a dream, this sure isn't very fuzzy.

"Remember that trip we went on last time?" Yashiro grins as we walk.

"Huh?"

"Remember? When I let you ride on my head?"

"Uhhh… Oh! Yeah, I remember now." That time we were flying through space. "How do you know about that?"

"Because I was there, of course."

Grrrr. That sounded kinda deep, but I know for a fact she isn't actually trying to be.

Yashiro's faint glow leads us to a hazy figure. One look at her clothes and bratty scowl and I recognize her instantly.

"Ugh." It's me from junior high—specifically, the early days before I mellowed out. "I don't really want to see this part."

But I can't turn a blind eye to it. Yashiro's heading right for her, and if I lose sight of Yashiro, I'll be plunged back into the impenetrable darkness.

"Ah, so this is Young Shimamura-san."

"That's one way to put it, I guess."

Frankly, she and I are *both* "young." We don't look all that different. But her expression is pointed, suggesting she's unhappy with something. She's wearing a basketball jersey and glaring in our direction. Sheesh, cool it. No wonder your friends all hate you.

"She appears to be angry."

"Yeah...I wonder what I was so upset about."

I was fighting a solitary battle, but against what? I try to remember, but it all blurs together. Mostly, I was dissatisfied with all the things that weren't going my way, so I worked hard to fight it and tried to overcome it. Friendships, sports, schoolwork, parents... These were all obstacles that I plowed straight through.

Then Preteen Me passes her basketball to me. It catches me off-guard, and since I can barely see, I end up dropping the ball. The pass was so fast and hard, it makes me want to snap at her. This is probably how my old teammates felt whenever I passed the ball to them out of the blue. The thought saps me of any desire to criticize my younger, more reckless self.

Junior high sucked, and Preteen Me did the best she could.

"Gee, thanks for digging all that up again."

This period of my life was prime humiliation fodder. It gave rise to a feeling of intense self-consciousness that thickened and thickened, then slowly hardened, then dried, until eventually I turned into...*this*. When I walk past, I half-expect her to spit at me, but instead, she lets me go. Still, I'm sure she's disappointed by the person I've become.

"Blegh, kill me."

"How come?"

"Then again, if I hadn't burned out back then, I wouldn't have softened up."

And so the Cryptid from Planet Lazy was born. Wait, am I a cryptid or an alien? Whatever. My point is, Preteen Me was trying to do the right thing.

Life is always a battle—in my case, an eternal struggle with my archnemesis, laziness. I know I can't run from it forever, or else it'll come back to bite me. So yeah, my bitchy, cringey preteen self still has the moral upper hand. It takes courage to confront your problems, but the great thing about dreams is that no matter how much you whine and complain and suffer and generally make an ass of yourself, no one else will ever see it. You can be your true, unpolished self.

"You have a lot of time on your hands, don't you, Shimamura-san?"

Er...setting aside this one exception.

"Look, it's peaceful here, okay? What, you don't like dreams?"

"The sweets here don't taste like anything. What's there to like?" she scoffs.

"Yeah...I guess dreams *are* kinda bland." But if I had to guess, she probably doesn't mean anything deep or cerebral by that either.

Memories can never truly be sweet. They pierce deep into your heart. Of course, I can't deny that there's plenty of masochists who rejoice in that misery. But that's not the same thing as true happiness.

At this realization, my hands clench into fists, and I face off against what lies on the other side of the darkness. Gradually, even *that* begins to disappear. The darkness is being cleared away.

"Looks like it's time to wake up."

Dawn is breaking, and the obnoxious world of light is starting to show itself.

"So it would seem."

Yashiro shoots up to the ceiling, and I recoil. Hey! You can't just fly around for no reason!

"I shall await you on the other side. Don't forget the donuts...donuts...donuts..."

For some reason, her voice echoes. It feels like an eternal farewell, but I have a sneaking suspicion that when I wake up, she'll be right there in my house like she's moved in. Meh, I don't mind it.

"After all, she helps me out from time to time."

If I remember this when I wake up, I'll buy her a donut. She'll probably complain if I don't get her more than one, though.

Then I wake from my dream and forget my entire train of thought. Everything in the subconscious layer is thereby erased—from my world, at least.

"Forever" only lasts as long as I do. Eternity is finite.

I turn back and see a dog, and a kid, and another kid— precious souls I once hoped to share my life with. But even in their absence, I don't want to forget what they left behind. Something blooms in my chest when I think of them...something a bit more beautiful than what I'm used to. So I can only pray from the bottom of my heart that it will last for the rest of my eternity.

It felt like someone was squishing my brain. And so I snapped back to reality—back to life.

"Phone..."

What woke me was the sound of my cell phone ringing. Slowly, I sat up in bed. Luckily, the clock was right there against the wall, so I looked up at it...and realized that I'd somehow gone back in time an hour. I stared blankly for a minute, then realized: No, I hadn't gone back in time. I had slept for *eleven hours*. What a great start to the weekend. More importantly, however, my phone was still ringing.

"Yes, yes, I hear you!"

I was sure it was Adachi before I ever looked at the screen. Adachi had interrupted my scheduled thirteen hours of sleep and dragged me kicking and screaming back to the real world. I could vaguely remember that this had happened before, but unlike last time, I was actually excited.

My head was heavy from oversleeping, but as I rose to my feet and took a few steps, the haze gradually cleared away. Maybe my blood circulation was improving. My fingers were still a little tingly, though. It felt like I'd gotten a lot of sleep last night, and had a lot of dreams...but it was all jumbled together, so I couldn't remember what had happened in them.

Meh, probably nothing important. They were just dreams, after all. Normally, there was never any benefit to remembering them. But this time, I felt strangely at peace with myself. So if my dreams could help me keep my head up and face reality, then that was enough for me.

The real world was filled with inconveniences that I would inevitably have to confront, one at a time. The mere thought was enough to exhaust my will to live. But now I had someone around to help me. From now on, I wasn't alone. And for the time being, I was actually pretty okay with that. It tickled my heart.

"...Hello? Adachi? Yes, yes, I haven't forgotten about our d-date... Uh huh..."

To my ears, my voice sounded ever so slightly giddy. Would she notice? She was my girlfriend, after all. She always paid close attention.

Quietly, a tiny part of me prayed she wouldn't tease me too hard.

interlude **The World We Share**

AFTER I HEARD the planet would be destroyed in three days, I decided to take a two-day trip. I had never left the safety of my hometown, and I was curious to see how far I could manage to get before my time was up. No time like the present, right? So I rushed out of the house.

After two days of traveling, I figured I'd come back home and spend the third day with my family. The first day would be spent walking there, and for the second day, I'd walk back.

The trains weren't running, obviously, since the world was ending. They had stopped moving forward, and I respected that. But *I* wanted to keep going, so my only choice was to go on foot.

Why am I doing this? Am I happy with my life choices? Will tomorrow be a better day? As I walked along in silence, I asked myself each of these questions in turn.

Late that night, I saw a park up ahead and walked in. This was my finish line. I had never seen this park before, and while it looked no different from any other park, it was still uncharted territory. I had officially set foot outside of the realm of my day-to-day life, and I was feeling pretty okay about it.

It was there, at the dead end of my life, that I met *her*.

Like me, the girl was carrying a backpack on her shoulders. Evidently, she was headed in the same direction. We decided to forego the introductions.

"Did you pack a lunch or anything?"

"Umm...I've got some sweet snacks, if that counts."

We both lowered our backpacks and started trading food. The other girl didn't seem to have a set destination in mind.

"I'm not going anywhere specific; I was just walking. But now I'm tired, so I'm taking a break." Her inky black hair swayed in the night breeze, and her face in profile looked as fragile as thin ice.

"Well, I'm planning to go back home tomorrow."

"Interesting."

"You're not gonna go home?"

"No. I'm not going back."

"*Interesting.*"

"Are you copying me?" A tiny smile crept up on her face. She seemed as distant and chilly as the moon in the sky.

"If you've got nowhere to go, wanna walk to town with me?" I suggested. *No road is long with good company*, as they say, and I was bound to get bored looking at all the same scenery in reverse. So, since we had the opportunity, I figured we may as well make the most of it.

Her legs swayed as she chuckled down at the ground. "That sounds nice."

Maybe tomorrow would be a better day after all.

"Say, what's your name?"

The world was ending. This was my last chance to introduce myself...and my last chance to learn the name of someone new. In three days—er, two days—none of it would matter anymore. Regardless, I still wanted to know. Even if it turned out the prophecy was wrong, and we all died tomorrow instead, I still would have wanted to know her name.

If my destiny was to plunge into eternal sleep with the rest of the planet, then meeting her here was my destiny too.

To some, this was the distant future of humanity; to me, it was normal life. So when I heard that people from another planet were moving here, I didn't think much of it.

Why were the older generations all going gaga over some planet we couldn't even visit? Even my parents, who I hardly ever spoke to, were frequently seen glued to the TV. But as the fervor burned hotter and hotter, I regarded that planet with icy composure. *I* had other priorities—like college and the rest of my future. There was still so much I needed to figure out. Not like those alien immigrants were going to impact *my* life at all.

Then these aforesaid aliens showed up, and I just so happened to live in the rural town located next to the rocket landing platform, which meant I could get a glimpse of the procession as it passed through, so I decided to join the crowd for a day. Mostly because they'd canceled school in celebration of the "special event." Every channel on TV was talking about the aliens anyway, so if I was going to be bombarded with images of them either way, I figured I might as well get a look at them in person.

The roads leading out of town were all blocked off; security personnel were stationed all over the place while the crowds were pushed off to the sides, like stray grains of rice in a bento box. As I stood among them, I quickly remembered why I didn't like crowds to begin with: the body heat. But I had already come this far, and I couldn't be bothered to turn around and go back.

Everyone really wants to see these aliens, I guess. Haven't you all seen enough of them on the news by now?

They didn't have extra arms or legs, or mouths that stretched from ear to ear. Nor were they parasites that implanted their eggs in us. Appearance-wise, they looked nearly identical to the people of our planet; the only real difference was in the color of their eyes.

According to various scientific studies, our planets were the same type, so the stages of biological evolution had resulted in humanoid creatures in both cases. That was just how the universe worked, apparently. Now the scientists were researching why it worked like that. They spent entire days thinking about the same complex subjects that would give me a headache after five minutes.

Adults sure are impressive like that... Glad I'm not one of them. I didn't want my life to get any harder than it already was.

Time passed, and right as I was starting to get *really* thirsty, the alien procession finally showed itself: a line of top-down convertibles surrounded by what looked like pompous bodyguards. *Wow, it's like a parade...or maybe it is a parade?* There were a lot of them (well, less than a hundred, probably) and this was our one chance to see them in person. As it turned out, the news reports were right: they didn't seem to have any "alien" characteristics.

It was...kind of anticlimactic, actually. *Are we sure those aren't just regular humans?* Despite my misgivings, however, the crowds grew louder. I could only imagine how deafening it must have been for the aliens.

How did it feel to be on that side of the spectacle? Were they intimidated by our sheer numbers? The leader was riding in the car at the front of the procession, smiling warmly. *It must be hard for them.*

A split second later, I reeled from a hard impact to the chest—so hard, it knocked the wind from my lungs. In all my life, I had never been struck quite like this. And all because I made eye contact with a girl riding in one of the cars.

Was it the dazzling sunlight? Did something catch her eye? Was it the wind? The clouds? Whatever it was exactly, it all came together to create the perfect formula to make her look my way. And at that precise moment, I just so happened to spot her amid the rest of her group. And so our eyes met.

Everything about her seemed to glow white beneath the bright sunshine. Her hair was pale blonde, and her eyes were golden yellow. As we locked eyes through the crowd, it felt like I was gazing up at the sun from the bottom of the ocean. One look at those golden eyes and I knew it was a moment I'd never forget for the rest of my life.

As the car slowly rolled along, however, that moment quickly came to an end. The other girl turned away. But I kept watching. Long after she had vanished from sight, I kept staring after her in the direction the procession took her. The noise and heat of the crowd didn't even register anymore.

A dozen indescribable feelings swirled on my tongue. We were both girls, and yet...this thrill...this excitement... these contradicting feelings of deep satisfaction and aching hunger... It felt like I was being tied up in knots.

Because she was an alien, only a select few would be permitted to approach her—qualified adults with *certifications* or whatever. But on the flip side...all I'd need to do is get certified. I didn't need to travel to a distant planet. She and I shared the same world.

Now I had an idea of what I wanted to do in college... and I decided to get there as fast as I possibly could.

A few years later and now fully certified, I arrived at the alien residential zone. It was located in a nice, breezy area with lots of plants and scant few Earthlings. On second thought, maybe it was the lack of Earthlings that helped keep all this greenery intact.

Just then, I spotted the girl I was looking for. She was sitting out on the grass near her designated residence, staring into space and enjoying the breeze. Before this moment, my heart was dancing, but now it felt like a small iron ball in my chest. In contrast with this peaceful enclosure, I was deathly nervous.

As I approached, the crunch of grass underfoot alerted her to my presence. She turned and squinted her eyes. Her hair was longer now than it was the last time I saw her; the mere sight of those long golden threads was enough to make me blush. But those yellow eyes hadn't changed a bit. Like last time, they left me dazzled and dizzy.

Then her jaw dropped. We didn't exchange a single word the last time we met—only ever made eye contact from afar—and yet she remembered me, just as I remembered her. The feeling of dizziness intensified at the thought.

When I walked up to her, she turned in my direction and pushed herself up onto her feet. At her full height, she wasn't quite as tall as I was. I flipped open my phrasebook, but my eyes couldn't focus on a single word. It felt like someone had vacuumed all the language skills right out of my brain. Meanwhile, my vision began to spin faster and faster with no signs of slowing.

I said something, and she froze. Then she said something back, and I fumbled. We were both too inexperienced to express ourselves fluently. But with my phrasebook in hand, I attempted to introduce myself, then used gestures to explain why I was here. Her lips traced over my name, and I nodded. Then she introduced herself in kind. I couldn't make it out clearly, but...

"Uhhh... Wait, but..."

Was I hearing things, or did she say her name was *Shimamura*? Surely, that clothing store didn't exist on their planet...did it? I squinted down at my phrasebook in puzzlement. She must have found this funny, because she started laughing.

Her smile made my blood throb in my veins.

I closed my phrasebook. I had a lot I wanted to tell her, but for right now...I was just grateful to have found her again. My racing heart was proof that I had come alive.

While I was waiting for the subway train, my eyes wandered to the stairs. Amid all the other faceless corporate drones, I found myself looking for *her*—the woman who rode the same train as me every morning.

To be clear, we didn't take the train *together*. We always rode in different train cars. She was just a face I had come to recognize. Then yesterday, we ended up sitting next to each other, and something spurred me to ask her name. After that, we parted ways.

I didn't have her phone number, and we hadn't made any plans to see each other again. She wasn't my friend or anything. We barely even *talked*. But now, all of a sudden, I was scared. Scared that I should have tried harder.

To be fair, I wasn't sure whether she even *wanted* to be friends with me. There was no guarantee that my effort would pay off; most of the time, it didn't. But this time, I actually had hope.

As I was fretting over the minor details, I saw head-lights approaching from the end of the tunnel. *Maybe she's taking a different train today,* I mused to myself. But when I glanced up at the stairs one last time, I spotted her among a group of latecomers making a mad dash for the platform. *Oh!* I could feel myself smiling.

As the train loudly rolled to a stop, she finally reached the bottom of the stairs. Then she spotted me and froze. But after a split second of hesitation, she rushed over to me. The last step she took was more of a jump, like she was crossing over an invisible line. For a moment we smiled at each other, seemingly unsure what to say. But in the end, we skipped the pleasantries and bolted onto the train before it could take off without us.

The morning train never had any empty seats, so instead, we stood side by side. We didn't work at the same company, so there was no telling how long we'd be riding together.

"'Sup," she greeted me casually, after she'd had a minute to catch her breath.

"Yo," I replied. *Why are we talking like a couple of DJs?* "Were you, uh, running late today?" I gestured with my hands to indicate her close shave just now.

She twirled a strand of hair around her finger. "I kinda overslept."

"Ah."

"I'm just not a morning person."

"Gotcha."

The conversation, if you could even call it that, ended there. This was par for the course for me whenever I interacted with my coworkers; I preferred to keep everything cut and dried. But now that same brevity had me feeling nervous.

"Say, um..." She started to speak; I made eye contact through the reflection in the window pane. "I know it might be hard to coordinate since we don't work at the same place, but...would you want to grab a meal sometime?"

My arm stiffened as I clung to the hand grip. "You mean after work?"

"Yeah."

This time I looked at her directly.

"I know it's kinda random, but...I think we could be good friends."

She grinned innocently, like a little kid, and I could feel my eyes lighting up with excitement. "That sounds great." I couldn't explain why—it just *did*.

The only thing tying us together was a vague premonition of a future that could be...but the uncertainty of it was actually kind of fun. As "random" as it was, it was no more random than the rest of my life thus far. And yet, for some mysterious reason, I was feeling a tiny bit optimistic.

And so my heart swayed with the motions of the train.

On an unusually sunny Monday morning, I left my house. The thought of another school day had me yawning already.

"Um...g-good morning!"

Once again, I found her standing stock-still outside my house, as if she was my personal assistant. For a moment, I was tempted to thrust out my chest and start acting like a bigshot CEO, but instead, I decided to keep it locked away in my imagination.

"Ha ha!"

First thing in the morning and she was already as stiff as a board—I couldn't help but laugh. Her sincerity and dedication always picked me up when I was feeling low.

"Good morning, Adachi."

Of all the people living on this planet—people who come into the world and pass on from it without ever meeting me—somehow, it was Adachi who stumbled into my life.

Here in this world we all share together...

Out of all the encounters I would never have, she was the one who found me.

Afterword

I ALWAYS FIND MYSELF thinking about the true meaning of destiny. And during that process, sometimes I make amazing discoveries! But no matter how hard I try, I'm incapable of fully verbalizing what I've figured out. Perhaps it's a hard limit that mere mortals can't surpass.

Despite how frustrating this is, after some time passes, I'll inevitably find myself thinking about destiny all over again. I'm obsessed with the way in which interpersonal relationships begin and end. Perhaps this is *my* destiny... (They told me I'm free to write whatever nonsense I like in this section, so there you go.)

That reminds me—I hear I'm going to receive an award. Maybe they'll give me a "wrote a bunch of books for Dengeki Bunko" prize. At this point, I don't know the exact number of books I've published, but I owe my success to all you readers out there. And I owe it to myself too, of course. I only pray that we all continue to live happy, healthy lives.

Again, I'm at least partly responsible for my own success. If I didn't write these books, no one else would have, I can tell you that much.

I worked hard yesterday and all the days before that, and I'll be working just as hard from here on out. If I don't put in the effort today, then I'll only struggle harder tomorrow. Not that I'm opposed to struggling, as long as it doesn't put *too* much extra on my plate... Is such a thing even possible? I haven't found it to be the case yet. Maybe it's a myth. I look forward to finding out.

At the time of this writing, I suspect that this will be my last published release of 2016. I know it's a little early still, but I want to thank you all for spending the year with me. If possible, I hope to see you again next year too. By all means, keep reading *Adachi and Shimamura*, or maybe try one of my other works.

Alternatively, I wrote a glowing review of Eiji Mikage's debut novel, *Bokura wa Dokonimo Hirakanai* ("Closed Off"), so feel free to read that too. Or tell his fans to check me out. Win-win for everybody!

For the record, 2017 marks my tenth anniversary as a novelist, and I'd like to publish something to commemorate it if I'm able to. Oh, and I think Volume 8 is going to be the school trip arc, but I haven't decided where they're going yet. Where do high schools send their students these days? Will I need to fit a "day at the hot springs" story in there somewhere? I don't know. I'm utterly clueless, to be honest.

—Hitoma Iruma

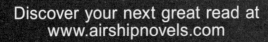